OMPLE

VAN MOE

CW00327670

Exclusive Distributors:
Book Sales Limited, 8/9 Frith Street, London W1V 5TZ, UK.
Music Sales Corporation, 257 Park Avenue South, New York, NY 10010, USA.
Music Sales Pty Limited, 120 Rothschild Avenue, Rosebery, NSW 2018, Australia.

To the Music Trade only:
Music Sales Limited, 8/9 Frith Street, London W1V 5TZ, UK.

Photo credits: Front cover: LFI. All other pictures supplied by Adrain Boot, LFI, Barry Plummer and Rex Features. Every effort has been made to trace the copyright holders of the photographs in this book but one or two were unreachable. We would be grateful if the photographers concerned would contact us.

Printed in the United Kingdom by Ebenezer Baylis & Son, Worcester.

A catalogue record for this book is available from the British Library.

OMNIBUS PRESS
LONDON · NEW YORK · SYDNEY

CONTENTS

INTRODUCTION

George Ivan Morrison was born in Hyndford Street, Belfast, on August 31, 1945. He grew up to be a legend: a songwriter of genius and an interviewer's nightmare, a grumpy old man and a transcendent soul singer.

Miserable and joyous, enervating and exhilarating, the music of Van Morrison has been with us for over 30 years; from his days as a sneering young soul rebel in the pounding Belfast R&B band Them, through a series of classic solo albums on which his reputation was built during the late Sixties and early Seventies ('Astral Weeks', 'Moondance', 'His Band And Street Choir', 'Veedon Fleece'). Van's music has taken us up to the mountain top, and rarely dips into the valley below.

On into the Nineties, Van also became the only star of the rock'n'roll era to receive an Order of the British Empire medal solely for his contribution to music – The Beatles' MBEs were for exports, while Geldof and Cliff were honoured for their charity work.

Surly and uncommunicative in inter-view, Van Morrison is one of the few rock stars – a title he bitterly resents – who literally lets his music do the talking for him. Such is his antipathy to inter-view that in 1974 Morrison instructed his then record company to publish a booklet – the ironically titled *Reliable Sources* – to obviate the process.

Unlike other artists of his stature, Van Morrison never goes out of his way to court the press. He will, grudgingly, accede to interviews to promote current product, but even then frequently stumps the journalist by not only throwing a blanket over "the past", but also refusing to discuss what he's just released.

Even an inoffensive passing refer-ence to Van as a "rock star" prompted a furious letter to Dublin's *Sunday Independent* in 1994. Morrison wrote: "To call me a rock star is absurd, as anyone who has listened to my music will observe. For the benefit of the unenlightened it is not my nature to be a rock star. What I am is a singer and songwriter who does blues, soul, jazz etc. If anyone is really interested, they would find I made my reputation as a blues singer in Belfast on the R&B scene, which I started in that city."

Ironically, three years previously when the Belfast Blues Appreciation Society had recognised this contribution to the city's musical heritage by unveiling a plaque on Morrison's Hyndford Street birthplace, Morrison had grumbled that it was "an invasion of privacy". But this combination of reluctance to discuss his work with outspoken public contrariness has only seen the Morrison myth grow.

As we approach the millennium, with a career stretching back over 35 years of rock'n'roll history, Van Morrison has positioned himself near the top of the tree. Few artists attract the devotion which attaches itself to Morrison. His career has seen wrong moves made,

errors which could have finished off lesser mortals, ill-judged musical collaborations, dubious albums and dodgy live shows… and yet Van Morrison survives, and thrives.

Then there are all the tantalising might-have-beens and almost-weres of his career, which further fuel the legend: was Morrison asked to score Francis Ford Coppola's magnificent failure 'One From The Heart'? Did he really record an entire album of material with The Crusaders? Why did he decline to produce his disciples Dexy's Midnight Runners? Why did he decide to "let the goldfish go?"

But transcending all this, is a body of work which stands virtually unequalled in the history of rock music, together with a critical reputation which is only enhanced the longer he stays at it.

Van fans span those who were first attracted by the earthy R&B of Them in 1964; those who were captivated by 'Astral Weeks' as the summer of love wound down; those who found Morrison's forging of Celtic mythology and rock'n'roll irresistible... Those have been with him all along the way. Then there are those who having heard his name dropped by their idols – be it Kevin Rowland, Bono or Bob Geldof – and have bent to pick it up.

Fans come from across the spectrum to pay homage, musicians acknowledge Van's influence, and since his Nineties rebirth in the company of Michelle Rocca, Morrison is to be seen in the company of the great and the good – Martin Sheen, Richard Gere, Liam Neeson, President Clinton. He even received the ultimate media accolade: finding himself impersonated on *Stars In Their Eyes*. His songs have cemented themselves – however much he denies it himself – as rock'n'roll standards, covered by stars such as Bruce Springsteen, Bob Dylan, Counting Crows, The Waterboys, John Mellencamp, Patti Smith and Rod Stewart,

The dichotomy for long–time Van fans comes in reconciling the uplifting, transcendent nature of their hero's music with the truculent and frequently abusive reality of The Man in his confrontations with the press. Being a fan of Van Morrison has never been easy. You go along for the ride, and accept whatever he is willing to slip your way. Most times, the quality of the music is unique and inimitable, a searing hybrid of folk, jazz, soul, blues, rock'n'roll... a melange of keening, questing lyrics, all topped off by that wild and utterly distinctive voice.

It's a hazardous, see–saw experience. In the Eighties, when Van was in residence at his favoured London venue for four or six nights, you could almost guarantee that half the shows would be sublime: a musical evening where Morrison would push himself and his music to the limit, teetering on the edge of revelation, and taking you with him to the brink. Other nights, Morrison would deliver a perfunctory show: mumbled ruminations into the microphone, a run through his latest album, with a few off–hand "hits" thrown in for good measure, a grunted "Good night", and off he went.

But that is the point of live music. You

can sit in an aircraft hangar somewhere on the outskirts of any town, and watch your favourite band from a distance, running through all their hits with syn-thesised, note–perfect precision, and then go home with your souvenir T–shirt and programme to remind yourself that you had been out to see them rather than staying home and playing the albums.

Live music, rock'n'roll (soul, R&B, call it what you will) in concert is about the moment, that sublime, unique moment, when the performer unites with his audience, and the mood of the room matches the onstage fervour, and the two mesh, like velcro. That moment (or in Morrison's case, moments) makes live music an indescribably vivid and unforgettable experience. Van Morrison has been playing music and creating those moments all his adult life. Like Bob Dylan, Bruce Springsteen, Richard Thompson and John Lennon, music is all he has known.

You can begin to understand the bitterness and bile which Morrison

unloads on the music industry and the media when you consider that for nearly 40 years, Van Morrison has been out there doing it. But then, it was what the boy always wanted.

George Ivan's dad stacked the family home with Wild West novels. Much later Van would say he didn't read Yeats until he'd written 100 of his own songs, claiming William Blake as the most influ-ential poet he had ever read. Throughout his recorded career, Morrison would namecheck the writers who he claimed had influenced him while he was growing up in Belfast – Kerouac, Rimbaud, Eliot, Joyce.

Music, however, was at the centre of the Morrison household. Van remem-bers his father George, who died in 1990, as "a collector, there were proba-bly only ten big collectors in Belfast... all the gospel stuff: Sister Rosetta, Mahalia Jackson, all the traditional jazz things: Bunk Johnson, Kid Ory, early Armstrong. My father also had all the swing band stuff: Tommy Dorsey, Artie Shaw, Harry James. He had Charlie

Parker's first record".

What was remarkable about George senior was not simply his sophisticated musical perception – few fledgling "rock" stars had the benefit of such a firm musical grounding as Van Morrison – but his ability to obtain records by the likes of Charlie Parker, Hank Williams and Leadbelly in the dour Belfast of the mid–Fifties.

Of all the ocean of influences swimming around in those formative years, when asked years later, Morrison stated emphatically: "Leadbelly was not an influence. Leadbelly was THE influence".

Van grew up in Belfast in a time long before "the troubles". By the time Belfast burst into bloody civil war and saw its streets patrolled by the British Army, Van like many of his countrymen before him, had long gone across the Atlantic Ocean.

George Morrison was a shipyard worker at the Harland & Wolff yard, at a time when Belfast was one of the UK's centres of shipbuilding. Van's mother Violet had lived at 125 Hyndford Street since she was nine. George Ivan was their only child, and true to the tradition of only children, he was a solitary, reclusive child, withdrawing into the world of literature and the ever–present music. Van was close to both his parents, and when he was living in Marin County in California in the mid–Seventies, George & Violet Morrison moved over to be closer to their only child and grand–daughter. Appropriately, for George, the Morrisons' time in the States was spent running a record store. His father bought Van his first guitar aged 12. Before long Van was practising hard, and in the wake of the Lonnie Donegan boom, forming skiffle groups with neighbours. Not long after Van became fascinated by the saxophone and took lessons.

He began playing professionally aged 15, at Belfast halls like The Hut and Brookborough Hall in pre-Them outfits with names like The Sputniks, The Thunderbirds, The Four Jacks, The Javelins; all playing the current hits by

Johnny Kidd & The Pirates, Cliff Richard & The Shadows or Jerry Lee Lewis. The first song he remembers writing was 'I Think I'm In Love With You'.

"I started doing this because I thought it was a job," Morrison told Chris Salewicz in 1987. "I had a choice. I was an apprentice engineer. And I thought, I don't want to be an apprentice engineer, I'd rather be a musician. How do you become a musician? You learn music and you study and you work hard, and you become a musician. It's a job. And the bottom line is that this is a job. I'm not doing it because I want to be on *Top Of The Pops*. Or because I want to do a big American tour. I've done those things... I got into it because it's a job."

Besides being an apprentice fitter, Van Morrison's day jobs had included being a window cleaner, as clearly recalled in a song – aptly entitled 'Cleaning Windows' – over 20 years later.

By 1960, Van was saxophonist with a showband called The Monarchs. In the predominantly rural Ireland of the early Sixties, with television a dream and cinema a city luxury, that uniquely Irish institution, the showband flourished and made a healthy living playing at the weekly village dances all over the province. "The promoters hated 'guitar, bass and drums' groups," Van recalled to *Now Dig This* magazine in 1991. "You had to have a horn section... All the showbands had horn sections and a lot of them were really good, like The Royal Showband, The Dixielanders, The Swingtime Aces...".

The Monarchs crossed to the mainland in 1962, working in Scotland before moving down to the bright lights of London, where – in the time–honoured tradition – they dutifully starved. Then, in the wake of The Beatles and a dozen other Liverpool groups, The Monarchs went over to Germany, where the beat boom was really booming.

It was at The Storyville Club in Cologne that Morrison began to find his own musical voice – besides enthusiastic German teenagers, the audiences were made up of American servicemen from nearby bases who wanted hard-edged R&B played loud and played long. The Monarchs gave them what they wanted and served a gruelling apprenticeship, playing eight-hour sets, seven nights a week.

One night when they were playing at The Storyville, The Monarchs were seen by a CBS Records' producer, who liked what he saw and heard and whipped them into a local studio. There, for a flat fee, Van Morrison made his recording début, playing saxophone on the gloriously titled 'Boozoo Hully Gully', backed by 'Twingy Baby'.

When 'Boozoo Hully Gully' predictably failed to give him his crack at the title, the teenage Van Morrison returned to Belfast with his tail between his legs. However, aged only 19, Van now knew that he wanted a career in music more than he wanted to be an apprentice fitter. In his head, he still heard the music he had created onstage with The Monarchs in the more frenzied milieu of Cologne, and he desperately

wanted to recreate that R&B fervour in his native Belfast. However he also recognised that he could never do it from within the showband formality of The Monarchs on their home turf.

So on his return to Belfast, Van Morrison put together a group of like-minded Belfast blues and R&B fanatics. They became Them. Them were the first outfit really to alert people to the potential of the stocky little singer.

The success of The Rolling Stones, The Yardbirds and The Animals, had already alerted record companies to the commercial potential of the fiery new Rhythm & Blues music. The fact that it was white-boy blues ensured a wider audience than that reached by the black originators of R&B. But back in the early Sixties, even after the success of The Beatles, record companies were still London-based and London-orientated. To the men of Decca and Parlophone, Belfast was a foreign country.

The turbulent career of Them, and the record company chicaneries in which the band found themselves embroiled, permanently soured Van Morrison's opinion of the industry which was to provide him with a living for the rest of his life.

Them came and made their mark, then were gone, like dozens of other regional phenomena during the heady days of the British Beat Boom. Disillusioned by the way Them's original devotion to R&B was compromised, tired of the endless slogs up and down the M1 motorway, bitter at the way the band had been ripped off, Morrison slipped back to his parents' home in Belfast.

Quietly determined not to return to life as an engineer or window cleaner, Van stayed in his room, and performed a series of his own songs into the family's tape recorder. That tape found its way into the hands of former Them producer and author of 'Here Comes The Night', Bert Berns. It was Berns who supervised Morrison's career between Them and 'Astral Weeks', and it was Berns who produced what was technically Morrison's first solo album, a fact which Van has constantly disputed.

'Blowin Your Mind!' may have been Van Morrison's first solo album release, but like David Bowie's eponymous début, the tracks have been so endlessly recycled – to the artist's very public distaste – that it is now little more than a footnote to his career. Assembled as an album by Bert Berns, without Morrison's knowledge or approval, 'Blowin Your Mind!' consisted of eight potential singles and B-sides, which Van had cut at Bang Records during 1967, simply glued together as a cash-in album, and quickly rushed into the shops to capitalise on the success of the 'Brown Eyed Girl' hit single.

Like "The Man" himself, I will take 'Astral Weeks' as the real starting point of his solo career, but more details of his work with Them and Bert Berns can be found in the chapter on compilations at the end of this book.

"That first album was four singles, it wasn't an album. Berns didn't think in terms of albums," Morrison told Sean O'Hagan. "He wanted me to record four singles and I went to New York and recorded four A-sides and four B-sides and that was an album. But there was no conscious thinking that this was an album. So really, my first album was 'Astral Weeks'."

ACKNOWLEDGEMENTS

Thanks to Johnny Rogan's 1984 Van Morrison biography, now criminally out of print; Ritchie Yorke's partisan but nonetheless revealing 1975 'Into The Music'; and Steve Turner's 1993 appreciation 'Too Late To Stop Now.'

Thanks, as ever, to Sue; Cassandra at Polydor; Quinton Scott at WEA and Simon Gee at Wavelength. Finally, thanks to Johnny Rogan, Gavin Martin, Stuart Bailie and Peter Hogan, for not writing this book.

Wavelength is a Van Morrison-tastic quarterly fanzine. Four issues every year keep you up to date on Van's music, gigs and hats. Worldwide subscription details from *Wavelength*, PO Box 80, Winsford, Cheshire, CW7 4ES, UK. You can also try contacting them at wavelength@netcentral.co.uk

VAN MORRISON ASTRAL WEEKS

ASTRAL WEEKS

(CD: WARNER BROS 246 024; RELEASED NOVEMBER 1968)

Astral Weeks' has been cemented into the pantheon of "All-Time Great Rock Albums" for nearly 30 years. Van Morrison was only 23 when he created this stunning and seamless album, and given the traumas which surrounded its recording, it is all the more extraordinary that each time you hear it, you are struck afresh by the serenity which 'Astral Weeks' seems to offer.

Timeless and transcendent, 'Astral Weeks' remains as fresh and enchanting on CD today as when it was first released on vinyl in 1968. At once both inscrutable and enticing, 'Astral Weeks' arrived – sandwiched by two rather more hard-edged phases of Morrison's career – between the break-up of Them and the brassy, R&B fuelled 'Moondance'.

The album which effectively began Morrison's solo career has baffled and enchanted successive generations since its release; for while it is frequently cited as a seminal rock album, 'Astral Weeks'' actual connection with "rock'n'roll" is at best tangential.

Warner Bros were becoming wary about the time (and more to the point, the money) that rock musicians spent in the studio bringing their dreams to life. Musical statements and philosophies were all well and good, but following The Beatles' 'Sgt Pepper...' the previous year, which had been £40,000 and six months in the making, record executives were growing increasingly suspicious of rock's ever-inflating sense of self-importance. After all they reasoned, that first Beatles' album had been recorded in one day, hadn't it?

To ensure that Morrison didn't dither, the musicians who accompanied him on 'Astral Weeks' were drawn largely from the more reliable world of jazz. Drummer Connie Kay came from The Modern Jazz Quartet, while bassist Richard Davis had served a spell with Miles Davis and guitarist Jay Berliner had worked with Charlie Mingus. 'Astral Weeks' was recorded in an incredible 48 hour burst at New York's Century Studios in September 1968, the horns and strings were overdubbed later.

Morrison himself is appropriately vague about this enigmatic album. However bassist Richard Davis has shared his more lyrical memories of the recording sessions: "You know how it is at dusk, when the day has ended, but it hasn't? There's a certain feeling about the seven to ten o'clock session. You've just come back from a dinner break, some guys have had a drink or two, it's this dusky part of the day, and everyone's relaxed. Sometimes that can be a problem, but with this record, I remember that the ambience of that time of day was all through everything we played."

It is the very refusal of 'Astral Weeks' to be pinned down and classified which has helped ensure it such legendary status. A heady mix of Celtic folk, American jazz, and R&B, all caressed and coalesced by Morrison's haunting lyrics.

Morrison did claim that 'Astral Weeks' was originally envisaged as "a rock opera" with "a definite story line". The mind, she boggle. Just what did Morrison have in mind for this story line? However, subsequently he refuted the opera angle, at the same time confusing matters further by stating that "the approach was operatic".

Certainly the songs on 'Astral Weeks' were steeped in the Belfast of Morrison's adolescence. Cyprus Avenue – close to Hyndford Street where Van was born, the train "from Dublin up to Sandy Row" and the evocation of Fitzroy Avenue, were all familiar territory from 'Madame George'. When it came to recording the album in New York, it was almost as if Morrison were recreating the city of his childhood in exile ("the childlike vision creeping into view..."), in the same way that James Joyce had evoked Dublin from Switzerland 40 years before.

"To me, Cyprus Avenue was a very mystical place," recalled Van later. "It was a whole avenue lined with trees, and I found it a place where I could think... You could walk down Cyprus Avenue and there was nobody there. It wasn't a thoroughfare. It was quiet, and I used to think about things there." For a long time, Belfast's prosperous Cyprus Avenue was also home to the Reverend Ian Paisley.

Morrison had written the bulk of material for the album while at home in Belfast between mid-67 and autumn 1968. Still signed to Bert Berns' Bang label, Morrison worked out unsatisfactory brassy versions of 'Beside You', 'Madame George' and 'Ballerina'. When the songs were re-recorded after Van signed to Warner Bros, the overall feel of the songs and the general direction of the ensuing album became altogether more contemplative, acoustic and string-driven.

Though written largely in Belfast, 'Astral Weeks' was recorded in America, where Morrison had made his home by the time of the album's release. It is perhaps that sense of "too long in exile" which lends the album its distance and feeling of timeless dislocation.

The core of 'Astral Weeks' lies in three lengthy songs – the title track, 'Cyprus Avenue' and 'Madame George' – "stream of consciousness things" according to Morrison – which account for over half the album's total playing time. This was the sound of rock music flexing its muscles, an album like 'Astral Weeks' helped liberate pop from the shackles of the three minute song. In the hands of someone as eloquent and capable as Van Morrison, late in 1968, anything truly did seem possible.

'Astral Weeks' itself sets the scene. As Van sings: "If I venture in the slipstream...", the song becomes a slipstream, a shuffling, percussive, deftly-plucked flow along the lines of Van's musical dreams. 'Cyprus Avenue' has Van hypnotised and "conquered in a car seat", recalling the tree-lined street near his Belfast home. The childhood fragments are somehow heightened by the resonant bass and baroque harpsichord.

For all its status as a classic album

there is some dead wood on 'Astral Weeks': 'Beside You' is forgettable, while 'Sweet Thing' is only enlivened by slashing strings that sweep in like bursts of rain.

'The Way Young Lovers Do' is perky and not too far removed, in style or length, from the buoyancy of 'Brown Eyed Girl'. But 'Ballerina' tries too hard to evoke a mood, and soon slumps into lethargic meditation. The abiding interest of 'Slim Slow Rider' is in Van's recollections of Ladbroke Grove rather than its unconvincing acoustic blues.

Undeniably, the album's cornerstone remains the haunting and resonant 'Madame George'. All these years on, the song remains one of rock's most atmospheric and beguiling moments. Epic and inscrutable, 'Madame George' has baffled fans since its recording, and Morrison himself has chosen to shed little light on its origins. "'Madame George' was about six or seven different people, who probably couldn't find themselves in there if they tried." Morrison has denied the

song is about a drag queen, but helpfully compared it to "a Swiss cheese sandwich". Marianne Faithfull, who covered the song on the 1994 Van tribute album, claims to know the real story, but she's not telling...

Much of the enduring appeal of 'Madame George' comes from the way Morrison constructs the song's brooding atmosphere: his vocal is trance–like, while all around, a deftly–plucked bass, piping flute and lightly brushed drums lay down a mosaic. A mood piece, 'Madame George' shifts gear as the strings form a wash of tears, and the cymbals tap as Morrison finally bids his muse adieu.

Half a decade later, Morrison looked back and admitted to Ritchie Yorke without too much pushing, that of all the 70 or so songs he had written to date, 'Madame George' was the one he enjoyed most: "Definitely, 'Madame George', definitely. I'm just starting to realise it more and more. It just seems to get at you... it just lays right in there, that whole track. The vocals and the instruments and the whole thing. I like that one."

In a straw poll conducted by Warner Bros in 1989, Bono, Tanita Tikaram, The Proclaimers and Shane MacGowan all selected 'Astral Weeks' as their favourite Van album. While in 1996, Joan Osborne cited it as her all–time favourite record "because it tastes good".

On its release, 'Astral Weeks' was compared with Dylan's 'Blonde On Blonde', The Doors' 'Waiting For The Sun' and Love's landmark 'Forever Changes'. Not everyone was initially captivated though; in his *NME* review, Nick Logan found 'Astral Weeks' wanting: "The album is as far removed from Them as possible, Morrison sounding for all the world like Jose Feliciano's stand-in... The songs themselves aren't particularly distinguished, apart from the title track, and suffer from being stuck in one groove throughout."

In his adopted home of America though, where the shadow of Them didn't loom so large, Van Morrison was to find a warmer welcome. *Rolling Stone* selected 'Astral Weeks' as its album of the year, saying it "sounded like nothing else in the pop music world of 1968".

Even today, nearly 30 years on, 'Astral Weeks' retains a unique place in rock history. Few subsequent albums (maybe Nick Drake's 'Bryter Layter', perhaps The Band's second album, possibly Bruce Springsteen's 'Nebraska') have so effortlessly evoked a time, a place and a mood as 'Astral Weeks'.

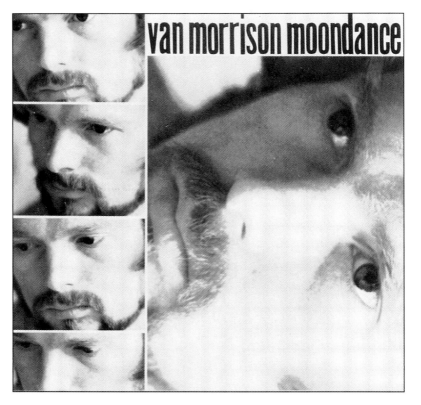

van morrison moondance

MOONDANCE

(WARNER BROS 7599–27326–2, FEBRUARY 1970)

Looking back, Morrison has few sentimental memories of the Golden Sixties. Talking to fiancee Michelle Rocca in 1995, Van laid the blame firmly at the feet of the writers: "This mythology, invented by rock writers, that started with *Rolling Stone* in America, and then it's developed now into your *Q* and *Mojo*... they've got a second-hand version of what was started in the Sixties. These writers, they call themselves rock critics, and they developed this mythology. It didn't actually exist. It was invented. And then the musicians and the artists wanted more publicity, so they fell in line and they played the game. So that's how the mythology developed – you've got the thing itself and then you've got the mythology of the thing."

But at the time 'Moondance' was released, looking back was still a long way in the future. Recorded at the end of the Sixties and released at the beginning of the Seventies, 'Moondance' confirmed emphatically that 'Astral Weeks' was no flash in the pan.

Appropriately for the beginning of a new decade, the album had Morrison sounding confident and looking more assured – the selection of cover portraits featured a bearded Morrison who appeared authentically poetic and suitably intense.

If the appeal of 'Astral Weeks' had lain in its acoustic, folk roots, the strengths of 'Moondance' were the album's overall brass tones, which stridently conveyed Morrison's enthusiasm for jazz.

There was a feeling of confidence on 'Moondance' which built on the tentative odyssey undertaken by 'Astral Weeks'. This time out Morrison was working with a band rooted in rock, among them musicians like Jack Schroer and John Platania, who would feature regularly in Morrison ensembles over the next few years.

'Crazy Love' and 'Brand New Day'

boasted the soul singing of Emily Houston, Judy Clay and Jackie Verdell, which added another strand to Morrison's already rich musical tapestry. The original side one of 'Moondance' (tracks one to five on the CD) is arguably the strongest of any in the Morrison canon, and a strong contender for one of the best ever opening sequences in rock'n'roll.

'Moondance' too was recorded in New York, conveniently for Morrison who was then living with his wife Janet in upstate Woodstock.

The inherent strengths of 'Moondance' were almost swamped by the flood of album releases throughout 1970. While Bob Dylan and The Beatles revealed their feet of clay on 'Self Portrait' and 'Let It Be' the year also saw 'Led Zeppelin III', John Lennon's 'Plastic Ono Band', James Taylor's 'Sweet Baby James', Creedence Clearwater Revival's 'Cosmo's Factory', Neil Young's 'After The Gold Rush' and The Band's 'Stage Fright'.

It was The Band to whom Morrison deferred musically, like everyone – musicians and non-musicians alike – Morrison had been bowled over by the gritty authenticity of The Band's first two albums, and their influence can be discerned on 'Moondance''s 'And It Stoned Me' and 'Caravan'.

In his exhaustive three part survey of Morrison's music in *Record Collector*, Peter Doggett confirmed the group's influence when he wrote: "What tipped the balance between eight-minute atmospherics and three-minute R&B songs? It can only have been the influence of The Band, who at the height of acid-rock experimentation asserted the virtues of ensemble playing and roots–based songwriting".

'And It Stoned Me' was the perfect opening shot, a song so in keeping with the times, following the year of festivals during 1969 – Woodstock, Isle of Wight, Altamont. There was a genuine frisson that this really was the dawning of the age of Aquarius. Here was the first flowering of an awareness of the environment. The overall agenda though was sex & drugs & rock & roll, and the mellow 'And It Stoned Me' seemed to ideally suit that. In fact, the song sprung from Morrison's memory of a pre–teen holiday, drinking water from a mountain stream, where time had stood still. 'And It Stoned Me' is one of rock's most atmospheric and sheerly pleasurable songs. The song's final verse still manages to contain a genuine sense of childish wonder.

For many, the abiding pleasure of 'Moondance' is the title track: a swinging pleasure which wouldn't have sounded out of place on a Frank Sinatra album ("when Sinatra sings against Nelson Riddle strings" Van was to sing three years later on 'Hard Nose The Highway'). 'Moondance' swings with authentic jazz fervour – beginning with the traditionally jazzy bass, drums and piano, before taking on board guitar and saxophones. Its swing feel has to do with the fact that Van began writing the song "as a saxophone solo". Morrison still features the song in concert – frequently as a springboard for lengthy solos – but the enduring appeal of this version is its economy.

'Crazy Love' is intimate and enticing, a love song from the heart, with the girls' voices ebbing and flowing behind Van. The song's softness shows a side of Van Morrison you rarely get to hear. It suggests unbridled affection for his new bride, for once free of ambiguity or complexity. The song's open and affecting nature is uncharacteristic of Morrison, but recalls the work of Paul Simon around the same time.

'Caravan' is a freewheeling memory of gypsy encampments. The song is also one of rock's best celebrations of itself, echoing the sheer unadulterated joy of hearing that sweet soul (R&B, rock'n'roll) music coming right at you out of your radio. Later, in concert (notably at The Band's 'Last Waltz') Van would underline his Celtic roots by emphasising the pronunciation of "radio". The brass kicks in, and carries Van along as he "la la las" his way to fade.

'Into The Mystic' is as fine a song as

any of the 500 or so which carry Van Morrison's name. As a composer, Van delighted in the song's ambiguity – he couldn't decide if the lyrics should read "Also younger than the sun" or "All so younger than the son..". The album version didn't contain a lyric sheet, the CD release did and plumped for the former. "I guess the song is just about being part of the universe". Although written in exile in America, there are familiar echoes of Van's Belfast boyhood, including a reference to the fog horn whistle that he would have been familiar with from the city's shipyards.

'Into The Mystic' has Morrison completely in control, he dominates the song, determined to rock gypsy souls and float forever into the unknown. His scat "too late to stop now" at the song's conclusion would, of course, provide him with the title for his first live album.

The remaining songs on 'Moondance' are by no means vintage Van – 'These Dreams Of You' is pleasant, and would have sat happily on 'His Band And Street Choir'; 'Everyone' makes rather too much use of Jeff Labes' clavinet and finds Morrison at a lyrical impasse while the concluding 'Glad Tidings' relays some rather unconvincing white funk.

The one remaining outstanding track on the album was 'Brand New Day', Morrison's own personal favourite from the album. Its sentiments seemed to slot in to the positive energy which had been so apparent at Woodstock, and beyond. 'Brand New Day' had its origins in Van listening to a Boston radio station and hearing The Band's version of Bob Dylan's 'I Shall Be Released'. Both songs deal with light shining into the darkness, precisely the sort of sentiments to celebrate and share at the dawn of a new decade.

Rolling Stone called 'Moondance' "an album of musical invention and lyrical confidence" and initial sales were encouraging, easily outpacing those of 'Astral Weeks'.

VAN MORRISON HIS BAND AND THE STREET CHOIR

HIS BAND AND THE STREET CHOIR
(WARNER BROS 7599–27188–2, JANUARY 1971)

Van Morrison's third album has always been undervalued by long-time followers. Maybe it's that inverted snobbery which has the fans loyally sticking by their favourite act during the years in the wilderness, but when said act is suddenly heisted by the mainstream, their loyalty is sorely tested.

'His Band And The Street Choir' was the album which saw Morrison stroll over onto Top 40 radio, thanks to the fiery opening track, 'Domino', which reached No 9 on the American singles charts at the end of 1970. In fact, 'His Band And The Street Choir' is chock full of potential hit singles, only two of the 12 tracks coming in at over four minutes, the rest hovering around that radio–friendly three minute mark. According to Morrison: "The record company was asking me for singles, so I made some – like 'Domino' which was actually longer, but got cut down. Then when I started giving them singles, they asked for albums".

Working with a tight rhythm section and bolstered by horns, 'His Band And The Street Choir' also featured the three backing vocalists (Emily Houston, Judy Clay and Jackie Verdell) from 'Moondance', as well as the "Street Choir", a chorus which boasted Morrison's wife Janet (was she really christened Janet Planet?) and Martha Velez, who went on to work with Bob Marley.

There is also a sense of community suggested by 'His Band And The Street Choir' – a group always had to be more than just a band back then – the inner sleeve of The Band's debut album had them posing with their families; Paul McCartney's début solo album of 1970 was a testament to the lovely Linda; John & Yoko were inseparable...

The pictures on the album sleeve show a happy, contented Morrison, although he was probably wise to stop wearing the dress. A measure of real contentment is evident from the photos, and Mrs Morrison's sleeve notes were presumably intended to emphasise that contentment rather than bring fans to the point of nausea: ("his life force pulling us all together... and, incredibly, I have seen Van open those parts of his secret self – his essential core of aloneness I had always feared could never be broken into – and say... yes, come in here. Know me").

Morrison himself was scathing about the album, which by all accounts suffered from problems during recording, problems which Van had managed to avoid on his previous two outings: "That album is like a kick in the head. It was originally a concept to do an acapella album – 'Street Choir' was to be an acapella group... But it didn't turn out; it all got weird".

In fact, 'His Band And The Street Choir' is one of Morrison's least "weird" albums ever. Kicking off with the irresistible riff of 'Domino', the album doesn't stall at all over the ensuing 11 tracks. Cut from the same cloth as 'Domino' are 'Give Me A Kiss (Just

One Sweet Kiss)', 'Blue Money' and 'Call Me Up In Dreamland': brassy, R&B fuelled workouts which fully demonstrate Morrison's love for, and assimilation of, black American music.

You can discern some of Morrison's self–confessed weirdness on tracks like 'Crazy Face', where Van in all earnestness, concludes with the announcement "Ladies and gentlemen, the prince is late..."; and 'Virgo Clowns', with its shifting, swaying rhythms and nagging chorus is undeniably one of Morrison's most off–the–wall songs.

'I've Been Working' clocks in at the Blues coalface; memorably included on the live 'It's Too Late To Stop Now', Morrison's original here is bolstered by a buoyant vocal, as well as some deft organ and horn inter–play.

'I'll Be Your Lover, Too' is pensive and angst–ridden. With Van dredging up some heartfelt emotion from the depths of his soul; this song indicates the direction he would take on longer – but not necessarily better – tracks over the next few albums.

'Gypsy Queen' keeps up the momentum, but the album begins to waver slightly with 'Sweet Jannie' and 'If I Ever Needed Someone'. Order is restored though with the concluding 'Street Choir', which begins as a clarion call for the Age of Aquarius (along the lines of 'Brand New Day' from 'Moondance' a year before) but drifts into a pensive reflection on the nature of exile, stardom and gravy.

Morrison rarely falters on this unjustly overlooked gem of an album. 'His Band And The Street Choir' has it all: surefire hits, tight-knit playing, assured vocals and Morrison's trademark sense of mystery. It was reviewed in *Rolling Stone* by Jon Landau, who went on to manage one Bruce Springsteen, ironically one of the "copycats" who Van would later rage had ripped him off. Back then, Landau recognised the album as "another beautiful phase in the continuing development of one of the few originals left in rock... the song he is singing keeps getting better and better".

'His Band And The Street Choir' is where Morrison finally patents his own inimitable brand of "blue-eyed soul". It is here that his perfect phrasing and his innate love of black music first shines through. This is the album where Van Morrison begins to find an authentic voice. Small wonder that John Peel said, with his tongue not that far from his cheek, that Van Morrison was the only white man he would allow to sing "Lord have mercy" on his show!

Van Morrison

Tupelo Honey

TUPELO HONEY
(POLYDOR 839 161-2, NOVEMBER 1971)

From the cover in, it looked as though all was well chez Morrison. But in fact, 'Tupelo Honey' was the album which marked the beginning of the end for Van'n'Jan. After five years together, Janet gave birth to a daughter Shana (who went on to sing with her father) but the couple separated in 1973, and divorced later the same year.

Prior to the split, the Morrisons had moved from Woodstock to Marin County, just north of San Francisco. The couple's former home was celebrated on the song 'Old Old Woodstock'.

Morrison and Janet had moved to Woodstock in February 1969, six months before the festival – which actually occurred at Bethel, half a hundred miles away from Woodstock itself. One reason given for Morrison moving to the tiny upstate New York artistic community was to be near The Band. The now legendary house "Big Pink" had been the group's home since 1966, when they in their turn had moved up there to be close to Bob Dylan.

The same year that saw the release of 'Tupelo Honey' witnessed one of Morrison's rare guest appearances – he duetted with The Band's Richard Manuel on the collaboration '4% Pantomime', which appeared on The Band's fourth album 'Cahoots'. Five years later, Morrison would be one of the special guests at The Band's farewell Last Waltz concert.

In the wake of Michael Wadleigh's epic three hour documentary of the festival and the triple album celebration, Woodstock became a magnet for those who hadn't made it to the actual event, but felt that some sort of truth was contained within the hamlet's leafy pastures. It was these seekers after the "truth" who so pissed Van off: "When I first went there, people were moving there to get away from the scene – and then Woodstock itself started being the scene... Everybody and his uncle started showing up at the bus station."

Marital difficulties aside, Morrison had little love for 'Tupelo Honey': "It consisted of songs that were left over from before, and that they'd finally gotten round to using. It wasn't really fresh. It was a whole bunch of songs that had been hanging around for a while. I was really trying to make a country & western album."

Morrison called in a few favours with familiar musicians – drummer Connie Kay was back working with Van for the first time since 'Astral Weeks', Gary Mallaber on percussion had worked with Morrison on 'Moondance', while John McFee was recruited from San Francisco band Clover to help out on pedal steel. Much later, Clover metamorphosed into Huey Lewis & The News, and backed Elvis Costello on his début album 'My Aim Is True', while McFee stuck around to help Costello go country on 'Almost Blue'.

There is an abiding feeling of warmed-up inspiration on 'Tupelo Honey', although this is only really evi-

dent on the old Side 1 (the first four tracks on the CD). The album's opening track, 'Wild Night', tries a mite too hard to replicate the impact of 'Domino' the year before. The song became a Top 30 hit for Morrison, but a 1994 cover by John Mellencamp & Me'Shell Ndegeocello got to No 3 in the States, making it the highest-charting Van Morrison song ever.

Meanwhile, back at 'Tupelo Honey', only '(Straight To Your Heart) Like A Cannonball' has the verve and panache Morrison so evidently wants to muster elsewhere. Even 'Old, Old Woodstock' isn't much of an epitaph for the singer's former home – the sole purpose of Van's visit is "to give my baby a squeeze". One of the implied themes of 'Tupelo Honey' is rebirth, but the way it's handled, at least on 'Starting A New Life', is perfunctory.

Even by the undeniably macho yardstick of the blues and R&B, 'You're My Woman' was decidedly out of synch with the prevalent Women's Liberation movement of the early Seventies. Van

can be too much to take when he gets all testosterone and butch, and he is at his swaggering, possessive worst on this track.

It is only on the fifth track, 'Tupelo Honey' itself, that things begin to show a marked improvement. Kicking off with the promise of all the tea in China, Van gets meditative and spins off on a near seven minute trip. 'Tupelo Honey' has Morrison at his ruminative best, spinning yarns and involving you in his world.

'I Wanna Roo You' is in part a homage to Van's father's Scottish roots. A breezy, rip-roaring slice of Celtic swing, the song acts as a perfect companion piece to the 'When That Evening Sun Goes Down'. It's on this song that you get to hear echoes of the country & western album Morrison originally envisaged.

The final four songs on 'Tupelo Honey' do seem to form some sort of suite, not in a forced "rock opera" thematic way, but rather linked by shared atmosphere, mood and spirit. The

album's final song is the irresistibly catchy 'Moonshine Whiskey'. Bibulous and brash, John McFee's pedal steel wails away behind Van's enthusiastic vocal. But just as he gets on board the train, Van gets all misty-eyed ("she's my Texas sweetheart, all the way from Arkansas..."), and he kicks the song back into gear. Where 'Moonshine Whiskey' seems in danger of losing it altogether, is when Van starts impersonating goldfish in the water; but common sense draws him back into the song, that curling guitar lick and an unforgettable riff.

In his *Melody Maker* review Richard Williams wrote: "'Tupelo Honey' sweeps away all fears because, although it doesn't represent a return to the anguish of 'Astral Weeks' or the sensual tautness of 'Moondance', it consolidates 'Street Choir''s sense of happiness and makes something worthwhile out of it."

Writing about 'Tupelo Honey' in 1984, Johnny Rogan noted that: "At a time when several of his contemporaries were being seduced by steel guitars and love-lorn whining, Morrison negotiated a fine

balance between the subtle and the sickly sentimental. In spite of its underlying romanticism and tendency to perpetrate the Morrison domestic tranquillity myth, 'Tupelo Honey' still sounds less calculating than Neil Young's 'Harvest' and less innocuous that James Taylor's 'Sweet Baby James'."

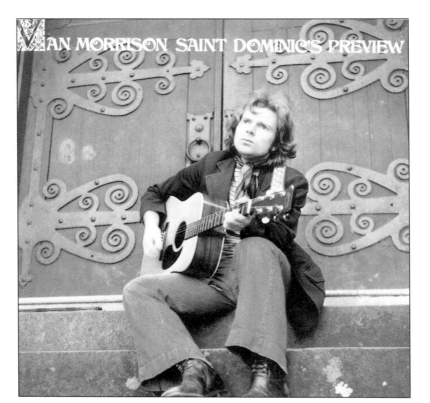

VAN MORRISON SAINT DOMINIC'S PREVIEW

SAINT DOMINIC'S PREVIEW
(POLYDOR 839 162-2, AUGUST 1972)

By the summer of 1972, Van Morrison had safely "arrived". His records may not have charted, but every release since 1968 was greeted with almost reverential acclaim from the press. In this Morrison was uniquely privileged, during the early Seventies there was no guarantee that albums from solo Beatles, The Rolling Stones or Bob Dylan would be accorded a thumbs up in the music press.

With Van Morrison though, there seemed to be an almost unnatural ability to consistently produce seamless albums. He was however still willing to experiment, and the run from 'Astral Weeks' to 1972 was – and remains – as near–perfect a sequence as rock music has any right to expect. Very few acts, either before (Bob Dylan, Paul Simon) or since (Elvis Costello, Richard Thompson) have been capable of matching Morrison's consistency.

Morrison had established himself as undeniably one of the most potent leading forces on the international rock stage by the early Seventies. He had managed to shake off the shackles of Them, and since 'Astral Weeks' had

ploughed his own unique and individual furrow. As the Seventies drew on, Morrison proved himself adept at moving along with every successive album, never more so than with his fifth solo album, 'Saint Dominic's Preview'.

The fresh breed of singer–songwriters who had emerged during the early Seventies – James Taylor, Loudon Wainwright III, Bruce Springsteen, Steve Goodman, John Prine, the "new Dylans" as the music press called them – all worked largely within the familiar format of guitar, vocal. Van Morrison had been there and done that. In a professional career already into its second decade, Morrison had proved that his musical abilities stretched far beyond

12-bar blues on an acoustic guitar. With a musical apprenticeship forged as a teenager, Morrison was adept on guitar, keyboards, harmonica and saxophone. That alone would have separated him from the majority of his singer-song-writer contemporaries, but from his earliest professional days, Morrison was also blessed with a raging lion of a voice which could cut across rock'n'roll, rhythm & blues, country & western, soul, folk, blues and all the way back again.

If there is any single element which could be said to elevate Morrison above his contemporaries, it is the full raging glory of that voice. Undeniably Irish, but drawing heavily on the vocal heritage of the American music which so inspired him, it is that voice which soars above the rest.

For Morrison fans, 'Saint Dominic's Preview' was remarkable on two counts: it was the first Morrison album to give full and free range to that remarkable voice – most notably on the two 10 minute plus tracks, 'Listen To The Lion' and 'Almost Independence

Day' – and it featured the track ('Almost Independence Day') on which Morrison became one of the first rock musicians to make full creative use of the Moog synthesiser .

'Saint Dominic's Preview' is another one of those frequently under-valued Van Morrison albums. In a sense, it is the Van For Everyone record, spanning the breadth of the man's musical interests: from the snappy R&B of 'Jackie Wilson Said (I'm In Heaven When You Smile)', through the keening folk-influenced title track; the bluesy cocktail jazz of 'I Will Be There', before culminating with the album's twin centrepieces, the A-Z compendium of 'Listen To The Lion' and the eerie, futuristic 'Almost Independence Day'.

Even the weaker tracks on 'Saint Dominic's Preview' ('Gypsy', 'Redwood Tree', 'I Will Be There') pound with Morrison's innately sure, soulful grasp. 'Saint Dominic's Preview' was the third album in succession to open with a brassy, up-tempo number which proudly displayed Morrison's debt to R&B, but none had done it better than 'Jackie Wilson Said (I'm In Heaven When You Smile)'. The object of Van's homage was a smooth-voiced singer, best remembered today for the use of his 1957 classic 'Reet Petite' in a 1986 TV advert. However by that time Wilson had been dead for two years having spent the last nine years of his life in a coma following an accident in 1975.

'Jackie Wilson Said...' is probably Van Morrison's best known song, thanks to the 1982 version which Dexy's Midnight Runners recorded as the follow-up to their phenomenal hit 'Come On Eileen'. Which prompts the question: is there any truth in the rumour that when Dexy's went on *Top Of The Pops* to promote the song, their request for an enormous backdrop of Jackie Wilson was met with a picture of portly Scottish darts supremo Jocky Wilson?

'Listen To The Lion' roamed far and wide on its odyssey. As it surges forward past the seven minute mark, the song possesses Morrison, and he rages and roars, battling with it, overwhelmed but not succumbing, as the background vocals gently repeat the title like a litany. Morrison grapples with the unreachable, unknowable concept. Like a great Viking longship easing into port, the horizon gradually becomes clear through the mist, as Van sings about sailing from Caledonia to Denmark. He riffs with the voyage, scat-singing, losing himself in a vocal he can only guess at and occasionally glimpse, "looking for a brand new start", all the way from San Francisco to New York City, and beyond. This was the nearest Morrison had come to reclaiming that trance-like state he achieved on 'Astral Weeks'. 'Listen To The Lion' was again helped by Connie Kay's drums, but this time the song was further enhanced by Bill Church's delicate bass and the gently strummed acoustic guitars of Van and Ronnie Montrose. Even by the inscrutable standards by which Morrison measured himself, 'Listen To The Lion' is baffling. Like the monolith in *2001: A Space Odyssey*, "its origin and purpose are a total mystery". 'Listen To The Lion' is imbued with that same mystery and magnificence, and once again gave Van a chance to indulge in goldfish impressions.

The song gave rise to an archetypal Morrison moment during a relatively low-key Van show at the Barbican sometime in the early Nineties. Van was special guest of The Danish Radio Big Band in a concert which was being broadcast live to Denmark. "Denmark" and "Danish" were the buzz words that night, so it was only fitting that Van should limber up with 'Listen To The Lion'. It was a brooding version, which built and built, right up until that reference to Denmark which would have sent every Dane home happy; except that this particular night Morrison decided to curtail the song and quit the stage before the anticipated reference to "sailing all the way to Denmark"!

The title track is one of Morrison's most riveting compositions. Ushered in by Tom Salisbury's sepulchral piano and organ, draped in John McFee's weeping

pedal steel, Bill Church's electric bass kicks it into touch. Lyrically, Morrison seems to have had the Thesaurus open at "cryptic", the lyrics of 'Saint Dominic's Preview' are as uncrackable as an Enigma code. P.F. Sloan – author of Barry McGuire's 'Eve Of Destruction' – is namechecked, as are Hank Williams, Safeway supermarkets, Edith Piaf's 'No Regrets', Joyce (James? Grenfell?), "chains, badges, flags and emblems..." and Belfast City too. There's also something in there about freeloaders at a record company shindig, but as to the actual meaning? Well you got me. All I know is that 'Saint Dominic's Preview' has all the greatness you associate with Van Morrison at his rampaging best.

I was always fascinated by just who "they" were, who were calling all the way from Oregon at the opening of 'Almost Independence Day'; then Van helped by telling Bill Flanagan in 1987: "I picked up the phone, and the operator said 'You have a phone call from Oregon. It's Mister So-and-So'. It was a guy from the group Them. And then there was nobody on the other end. So out of that I started writing 'I can hear Them calling, 'way from Oregon'."

Aside from the purposeful mystery with which Morrison fuels the song, 'Almost Independence Day' is remarkable for its haunting wash of Moog synthesiser, played by Bernie Krause. Krause had lent Moog mood to records by The Byrds, Beach Boys and Simon & Garfunkel by the time he came to work with Van Morrison, but the Moog was still largely the prerogative of progressive rockers like Rick Wakeman and Keith Emerson. Proper musicians remained wary of its electronic potential (for years Queen album sleeves would boast "No synthesisers").

Comparisons were made with 'Madame George', which Morrison predictably disputed. As far as the origin of the song, only Van knows. Its title suggests July 4, there are certainly references to San Francisco's Chinatown... mere coincidence that The Band's album 'Cahoots', on which Morrison had guested the previous year, featured a track called 'Shoot Out In Chinatown'? Morrison recalled the Moog player's involvement: "I asked Bernie Krause to do this thing of Chinatown, and then come in with the high part because I was thinking of dragons and fireworks. It reminded me of that. It was a stream—of—consciousness trip again".

'Almost Independence Day' is another of those marathon fishing boat—bobbing songs, with Van yearning for the safe lure of harbour, as he roves "way up and down the line". It is a song steeped in atmosphere and mood, from Morrison's wordless accompaniment to Ron Elliott's gracefully picked guitar which opens the song, through to the subdued howl which brings the song, and the album, to a memorable conclusion.

HARD NOSE THE HIGHWAY

(POLYDOR 839 163–2, JULY 1973)

Hard Nose The Highway' marked a period of confusion in the life and work of Van Morrison. Until now his professional career had been hallmarked by certainty and a sense of purpose, but separated from his wife and daughter, Morrison appeared to be drifting. Critics felt it to be significant that, for the first time ever on a Van Morrison album, not all the tracks were original compositions, 'Bein' Green' and 'Purple Heather' were both cover versions. What remained was a curate's egg of an album.

Morrison had appeared at club shows around his Marin County home with singer-songwriter Jackie DeShannon, best remembered for her Sixties songs 'Needles & Pins' and 'When You Walk In The Room'. She is credited as backing vocalist on the album's opening track 'Snow In San Anselmo', along with the Oakland Symphony Chamber Chorus. The two even recorded a single – 'Sweet Sixteen' – in 1972, but it remains unreleased. In 1979 another joint Morrison/DeShannon composition, 'Santa Fe', appeared on Van's 'Wavelength' album.

'Snow In San Anselmo' features Morrison's plaintive, high vocals, commemorating the first snowfall on the nearby community of San Anselmo in 30 years. A curious and compelling opening track, Morrison again deftly paints a portrait of a community, snuggling down as chestnuts roast on an open fire, they're safe and warm inside, which leads neatly into...

'Warm Love' which is one of those effortlessly charming Van Morrison love songs, with a third verse recalling the sentiments and mood of 'Brown Eyed Girl'. The song was a minor hit for Morrison in the States, "a boy and girl song... walking on the beach. It's a young song" recalled Morrison.

'Hard Nose The Highway' is one of the few songs whose origins Morrison has been willing to describe. Talking to

Ritchie Yorke, Van explained: "The first verse is an image of Frank Sinatra going into the studio and saying 'Let's do it'. He makes an album, then walks out and takes a vacation. It's an image of professionalism... The second image is of Marin County. It's becoming more professional, but it's a beautiful place... The second verse is... that kind of being weary with the scene... The second verse is about being depressed, but it doesn't matter because it doesn't make much difference anyway. The third verse is about record companies, promoters and all the business people in music...

"The theme running through the whole song is 'Seen some hard times', which I have. 'Drawn some fine lines', which I definitely have, and 'No time for shoe shines', when you're trying to make a living. That's about the whole thing."

'Wild Children' is the album's first major work, a weary reflection on the post-war baby boomers, like Morrison himself (born 1945), who had grown up

through the Fifties. It's a shopping list of idols and influences (Marlon Brando, James Dean, Rod Steiger, and perhaps more surprisingly, playwright Tennessee Williams). What stops the song being merely a list is a verse which opens and closes it, consisting of Morrison's evocation of the soldiers returning from the bloody conflict of World War II. Morrison admitted to Ritchie Yorke: "I think that where that song is coming from is growing up in another country and getting our releases through figures from America, like the American anti-heroes."

'The Great Deception' has Van railing against "plastic revolutionaries" and "so-called hippies". It's a tilt against the windmill of revolution, but it is rare for Morrison to be so specific in his targets: he is against artifice and hypocrisy, he is for the artist and his integrity.

'Bein' Green' was written in 1970 for the American kids TV show *Sesame Street*. It was sung by Kermit the Frog, who later split, and went on to lead The

Muppets. Eyebrows were raised at the idea of the, undeniably funky, Van Morrison covering a song which was originally written for a frog. Van justified its inclusion with the comment: "I think it's a good song for what it says about being green. That was just a statement that you don't have to be flamboyant".

The 10 minute 'Autumn Song' was obviously intended to be the major "statement" on 'Hard Nose The Highway', however it leaves the listener wanting. An unremarkable melody and half–hearted vocal don't help, but the overall fault lies in Morrison's determination to stretch such an insubstantial fragment into a magnum opus.

'Hard Nose The Highway' concludes with 'Purple Heather', a traditional song popularised by Belfast's McPeake Family. The song, also known as 'Wild Mountain Thyme', had already been recorded by The Byrds, Joan Baez, The Clancy Brothers and Marianne Faithfull. It was also Bob Dylan's concession to his UK audience, when he performed it at his "comeback" 1969 appearance at the Isle of Wight. Van's version is beautifully orchestrated and arranged, with a pealing piano played out against a waterfall of strings. Morrison loses himself in the age–old melody, seeming to drown before your ears in an ocean of strings and the haunting resonance of the timeless tune.

'Purple Heather' was a song Van would have been familiar with growing up in Belfast and covering it was an affirmation of his Irish roots. Placing it at the end of an otherwise unremarkable album proved to be a tantalising indication of what was to come.

VEEDON FLEECE

(POLYDOR 839 164–2, OCTOBER 1974)

Veedon Fleece' is the album which marked the real return to Van Morrison's Irish roots. He had effectively been in exile from his homeland since 1967, when he had left to go to America. Even his parents had left Belfast during the Seventies to move nearer to their only son .

The inclusion of 'Purple Heather' at the conclusion of 'Hard Nose The Highway' in 1973 may have been mere coincidence, but during 1974 Morrison seemed further to reaffirm his Irishness, with a series of shows in Dublin (though many were cheesed off that he ignored his home town up in the North). More decisively, the critics recognised Van's journey back to "a' things Celtic" in the songs which constituted his seventh solo album, 'Veedon Fleece'.

Right from the album cover – where Van is seen sitting nervously betwixt a pair of massive Irish wolfhounds – 'Veedon Fleece' resonates with Morrison's recent re–visiting of Ireland. Over the years, Morrison has dismissed the idea of any record cover bearing any relation to his life; but as with many albums which you have lived with for over two decades, the cover of 'Veedon Fleece' has come to reflect the music which is found within.

'Veedon Fleece' is another of those transitional Van Morrison albums, indeed it turned out to be his final record before a three year sabbatical. It was the first of his albums to invoke the mystic poet William Blake, and sent Van off on a spiritual odyssey from which he has yet to return. It is a record which has Morrison bridging the gap between lengthy, complex journeys like those he undertook on 'Astral Weeks' and 'Saint Dominic's Preview', and the more taut and disciplined songs ('Bulbs', 'Linden Arden Stole The Highlights') which recall the commercial highlights of 'His Band And The Street Choir'.

The Irishness apparent on 'Veedon Fleece' suffuses the album. A visit to

Ireland late in 1973 saw Morrison visit Cork and Killarney and pay his respects at the Blarney Stone. It was during that three week visit that he began writing the bulk of the material which would occupy 'Veedon Fleece'.

'Fair Play' was a rambling, unfocused opening, but the song slowly drew you in. Another Irish exile, Oscar Wilde, appears early on, but the running figure is 'Geronimo', almost certainly un–Irish, who Morrison keeps conjuring up. Further child–like visions crop up as Van echoes The Lone Ranger's unforgettable clarion call "Hi–ho Silver!"

Aside from being one of the best-ever Morrison song titles, 'Linden Arden Stole The Highlights' is also one of his most haunting compositions. Shadowed by a piano and covered by strings, Morrison tells of Linden Arden (outlaw? rebel? hero?) and his time spent taking the law into his own hands. Morrison truly lets rip on this short song, and the song's last line: "living with a gun", ushers in 'Who Was That Masked Man' a rather weaker variant of

'Linden Arden...'

Morrison's renewed interest in his Irish heritage finds further refuge in 'Streets Of Arklow', though quite what so impressed Morrison about this small County Wicklow town goes unrecorded in the song. The wandering gypsy is again evoked, remembered from 'Caravan'.

'You Don't Pull No Punches, But You Don't Push The River' suggested that Van had been going along to Great Song Title evening classes, or was Van simply a Jerry Lewis fan ('Don't Raise The Bridge, Lower The River' was one of the irritating comedian's film titles). The song is crucial in Morrison mythology as the first to demonstrate Van's growing interest in the work of poet, essayist and artist William Blake. Blake is in there with "the Eternals", the "sisters of mercy", and a trip out west.

'You Don't Pull No Punches...' is the song from which the album takes its title. Biographer Steve Turner speculated that the 'Veedon Fleece' was "Van's equivalent of the Holy Grail, a religious relic that would answer his questions if he could track it down", although later Turner recalls an encounter when he questioned Van about the title, only to be told "It doesn't mean anything. I made it up myself." The nearest we can come is the Golden Fleece of Greek myth.

'Bulbs' is the last great song on 'Veedon Fleece'. It's another of those criminally, critically under-rated, Van Morrison songs. Similar in style and subject matter (as far as I can make out) to 'Street Choir', with its references to exile from America; there's also something in there about an Atlantic sound, corroding batteries and a refrain about "standing in the shadows when the street lights all turn blue". Van is at turns endearing and gruffly intimidating here. There's an infectious riff, jaunty guitar and memorable melody. The surprise is that 'Bulbs' wasn't a hit when it was released as a single during the autumn of 1974.

'Veedon Fleece' wraps with the folk-leanings of 'Country Fair', a meditative piece, which strongly features Jim Rothermel's flute. The song pays lip service to Morrison's Irish renaissance, but was a desultory conclusion to an album which contained some of Van Morrison's most remarkable writing to date.

There was nothing here though to suggest that 'Veedon Fleece' would be the final Van Morrison release for three long years.

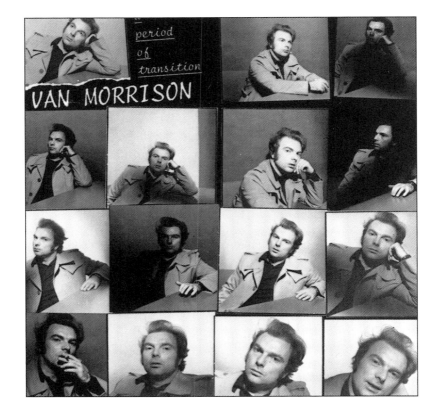

A PERIOD OF TRANSITION

(POLYDOR 839 165–2, MARCH 1977)

The period between 'Veedon Fleece' and 'A Period Of Transition' had seen the UK music scene tumble into the abyss of Punk. When Van Morrison had last released an album, the music press were generally sympathetic to the sort of laid-back, rootsy American music typified by Little Feat and The Eagles. They had a real reverence for old Van; he hadn't put a foot wrong since 'Astral Weeks' way back in 1968. Sure, he had faltered at times ('Tupelo Honey', 'Hard Nose The Highway'), but Morrison had always bounced back with his inimitable brand of blue–eyed soul, white R&B, jazz–tinged rock'n'roll. Call it what you will, the patented purveyor of that unique brand of music was, ladies and gentlemen, George Ivan Morrison.

Since 'Veedon Fleece' however, Punk had snarled its way out of the clubs and into the charts. Few of the old guard (Bowie, Dylan) had survived the shock of the new, but because of his refusal to play the media game, his reluctance to court favour and the intense, enduring, uniquely high quality of his music, Van Morrison managed to escape the wrath of all the young punks. His period of absence was rather the result of a life spent on the road.

Barely into his thirties, Van had been out touring for over half his life. For the first time in his adult life, Morrison found that music wasn't healing him: "I got to the point where music just wasn't doing it for me anymore" he told *The Guardian's* Robin Denselow. "It was a point I thought I'd never reach. I hadn't taken time off before, and something was telling me to knock it off a bit... The reason I first got into music and the reason I was then doing it were conflicting. It was such a paradox."

Steve Turner also had Morrison turning deep inside himself during his three year hiatus. With William Blake as his touchstone, Van began a spiritual odyssey, which took in Indian Yogi, Gestalt therapy, "spiritual friends", self–analysis and much, much more...

Between 1975 and 1977, Morrison also suffered from writer's block; for the first time in his career, he was failing at making the connection between himself and his muse.

In May 1976, Morrison took the extraordinary step of issuing a press statement to quell rumours that he was retiring: "I went through a lot of personal changes. There were a lot of things within myself that I had to sort out." The statement continued that Van was planning to move back to England after the best part of a decade in America, and that the direction his new music was taking was "roots... basic rock'n'roll".

While he was away Morrison undertook some recording sessions, including one with The Crusaders' Joe Sample, which led to the rumour that there were plans for a full-scale Van Morrison and The Crusaders album. Strong rumours persisted that Van had completed an album, to be called either 'Mechanical Bliss', 'Naked In The Jungle' or 'Stiff Upper Lip'. Only one song called 'Mechanical Bliss' ever appeared, as the

B-side of the single 'Joyous Sound', which was lifted off 'A Period Of Transition' in 1977. 'Mechanical Bliss' is surely the most bizarre work ever attributed to Van Morrison, a spoof comedy recitation, with Van sounding more like a stiff upper lip English aristocrat than The Belfast Cowboy.

Between 1974 and 1977 Morrison rarely broke cover. His most public appearance was in San Francisco in 1976, helping The Band bring it all back home at The Last Waltz. Morrison was one of the undeniable highlights, as commemorated in Martin Scorsese's fluid and elegant movie to commemorate the event. Van barnstormed his way through 'Caravan' and 'Tura Lura Lura (That's An Irish Lullaby)', high-kicking his way through the set.

Another guest at The Last Waltz was Dr John, who Morrison enlisted as co-producer and musical collaborator for his "comeback" album, 'A Period Of Transition'.

The anticipation was tangible, but on its release the album failed to match

most people's expectations of what a Van Morrison album should deliver. 'A Period Of Transition' is certainly lacklustre and in retrospect appears coldly calculating.

Opening with the leaden 'You Gotta Make It Through The World', much of the ensuing derisory 33 minutes, bears the dead hand of Dr John. 'Joyous Sound' was the last thing that anyone wanted to hear: Van Morrison sounding like an undistinguished Van Morrison parody. There was little to elevate songs such as 'Flamingos Fly' and 'Cold Wind In August', their titles were the best thing about them.

Only 'The Eternal Kansas City' approaches anything like the serene, triumphant plateaux which Morrison had previously reached. Its hesitant, choral opening allows a lengthy question, asking the way to one of rock'n'roll's favourite cities – The Beatles had tackled Little Richard's reworking of Leiber & Stoller's 'Kansas City' on 'Beatles For Sale'. Van's journey took him down jazz alleys, namechecking Charlie Parker and Billie Holiday, as well as noting "Bessie and Young, Witherspoon and Jay McShann".

This one song aside, there was little to commend 'A Period Of Transition'. But maybe it was an album Morrison needed to make in order to clear his writer's block and blow away the cobwebs.

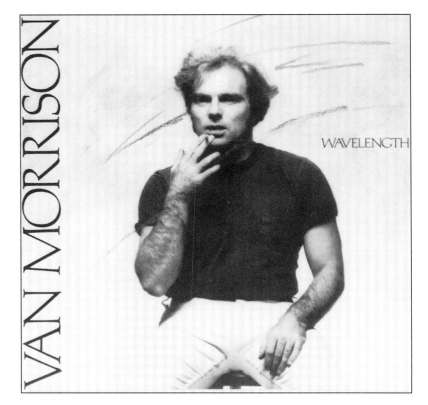

WAVELENGTH

(POLYDOR 839 169-2, OCTOBER 1978)

Wavelength' was everything that 'A Period Of Transition' had failed to be. From its breezy opening with 'Kingdom Hall', Van Morrison sounded confident and back in control.

His standing in the music hierarchy remained unimpaired as the Seventies wound down, Van was one of the few legends still flourishing. Punk had kicked a lot of preconceptions out of the window, and unlike other Sixties survivors (The Stones, Paul McCartney), Morrison had remained set on his own mysterious course, never trying to court favour with the new audiences who flocked to The Clash and The Jam. By 1978 the influence of Van Morrison's gritty, soul–tinged rock'n'roll music could be discerned in all manner of acts which had sprung to prominence in the Seventies, most notably Bruce Springsteen, Elvis Costello and Graham Parker.

There was still a sense of mystery surrounding Van Morrison: he hadn't toured properly in years, so few people who were now coming to appreciate the timeless beauty of, say 'Astral Weeks', had ever seen The Man play in the flesh. Van also rarely granted interviews, so the veil was hardly ever pierced by intrusive questioning.

When Morrison did break cover it wasn't a particularly rewarding experience. During 1977, in a half–hearted attempt to promote the desultory 'A Period Of Transition', Morrison agreed to be interviewed live on-air by amiable Capital Radio DJ Nicky Horne. It remains one of the most frustrating, brusque and pointlessly rude encounters ever aired. Morrison plainly didn't want to be there at all, and Horne was like a drowning man, watching his whole professional life flash before him, as Van Morrison grunted his way through the "interview".

A series of under-rehearsed club shows before keenly anticipatory press

did little to add lustre to his image. What Morrison needed to get him back up there was a strong album, and while 'Wavelength' doesn't make it into the classic Van canon alongside his first three albums, it is a marked improvement on 'A Period Of Transition', and better yet, indicated that there was still some life left in the old dog.

'Wavelength' was recorded at Richard Branson's Manor Studios in the beautiful Oxfordshire countryside. Musicians mustered for the album sessions included, on keyboards, Peter Bardens who had flitted through one of the innumerable line-ups which characterised Them. Another name from the past was Herbie Armstrong who Morrison had known as a teenager, when they had played in rival Belfast showbands. To bring the musical background up to date, The Band's Garth Hudson was also featured prominently on three tracks.

One of the weaknesses of 'Wavelength' is the album's over-reliance on the sweet as syrup backing vocals of Ginger Blake, Linda Dillard and Laura Creamer. Perhaps Morrison was inspired by the prominent use Bob Dylan had made of his three female backing vocalists, on the Street Legal tour that same year – Dylan had taken his lead from Bob Marley and The I-Threes – or maybe Van felt that this was one way to rekindle the magic of 'Moondance'. Overall though, 'Wavelength' contained just enough positive echoes of former Morrison glories, and at the same time displayed Van's ability to pull himself back from the precipice.

'Kingdom Hall' was the meeting place of the Jehovah's Witnesses, the religious sect with which Morrison's mother Violet had been closely involved while Van was a teenager in Belfast. The song is another of those punchy Van Morrison album openers which bodes well for what follows.

Songs such as 'Checkin' It Out', 'Natalia' and 'Hungry For Your Love' display little of the quality which otherwise runs through the album. It is when

Van gets riffing that 'Wavelength' kicks up a gear. As a straightforward story, 'Venice USA' wouldn't detain the casual listener long, but Van manages to infuse it with genuine buoyancy, even if it does eventually overstay its welcome by a couple of minutes. The melody combined with Van's scat singing help the song gain momentum, though the refrain "dum derra dum dum diddy diddy dah dah..." wouldn't cause W.B. Yeats any sleepless nights.

'Checkin' It Out' is a Van shopping list of spirituality, a tentative exploration of the "guides and spirits" which have helped the writer along his journey. 'Wavelength' itself is another of those Van homages to the comforting presence of the radio in his early life. The song's reference to the Voice of America recalls one of the few opportunities for rock'n'roll obsessed kids growing up in the BBC-dominated Fifties to hear authentic American rock'n'roll.

'Santa Fe' was left over from Van's association with Jackie De Shannon

around the time of 'Hard Nose The Highway', and would have sat happily on that strongly American influenced album. On 'Wavelength', the collaboration leads into a Morrison original, the gripping 'Beautiful Obsession', which is of interest for the way it has Van riffing on "let the cowboy ride" as the song fades. The cowboy is one of those leitmotifs which have wormed their way into the singer's subconscious, he shakes and picks away at them, like a sticking plaster which he can't quite lose.

'Take It Where You Find It' is a magnificent conclusion: an eight-minute plus meditation on his adopted homeland of America and his burgeoning spiritual awareness, all connecting on a sweeping, epic finale.

Whatever critical conclusions were drawn (*Melody Maker* were worried about the increasing Americanisation of Van Morrison) 'Wavelength' went on to become Morrison's fastest-selling album to date. Looking back with Bill Flanagan, Morrison called the album "a diversion. It was just to have a bit of fun

and go back to how it felt to play rock'n'roll... I think the fact that it was commercially successful really didn't have anything to do with anything... It was intended to be a bit less serious than my other projects."

VAN MORRISON/*Into the Music*

INTO THE MUSIC

(POLYDOR 839 603–2, AUGUST 1979)

I had a ticket for Morrison's show at the Rainbow in 1973, but was ill and couldn't make it. That was one of the shows which made it onto the live 'It's Too Late To Stop Now' set. "Unforgettable" was the buzz surrounding those '73 shows. It was not until he was touring in 1979 to promote 'Wavelength' that I first saw Van Morrison in concert; but by then his legend had preceded him and "entirely forgettable" was the impact he made live.

It was a grudging, half-hearted 50 minute set at the Hammersmith Odeon. The band were uninspired, Morrison was clearly reluctant to be there, and he spent what seemed like half the evening asking the audience to acknowledge the Caledonia Soul Orchestra – or whatever name they were labouring under at that time. Bitterly disappointed by the live performance, I put Van Morrison on hold. But my indifference didn't last long, and 'Into The Music' removed any lingering doubts.

The title of Morrison's tenth album, 'Into The Music', held echoes of his second, inevitably recalling 'Into The Mystic' from 'Moondance'. 'Wavelength' had already proved that when he buckled down and made music, he remained in a class of his own. 'Into The Music' more

than confirmed that.

Guitarist Herbie Armstrong was back on board, as were drummer Peter Van Hooke and saxophonist Pee Wee Ellis, who featured regularly in Morrison's bands throughout the Eighties. Eyebrows were raised at Van's decision to let Katie Kissoon handle the backing vocal duties. Along with her brother Mac, Katie had enjoyed a couple of UK hits in 1975, and although such chart-friendly material as 'Sugar Candy Kisses' didn't seem to sit happily alongside Morrison's intense, fiery, personal brand of rock'n'roll, something obviously clicked. The record has a more acoustic and folk influence in place of 'Wavelength''s brassy rhythms. Although recorded in America, the bulk of the material for 'Into The Music' was written while Morrison was staying in Oxfordshire.

Ellis' saxes and Mark Isham's trumpet made regular appearances, while the folk aspect of the record was emphasised by Toni Marcus' violin and the presence of the Incredible String Band's Robin Williamson on two tracks. In content too, 'Into The Music' sported its folk credentials, with songs such as 'Troubadors', and the musical setting of 'Rolling Hills'.

Otherwise, 'Into The Music' was much as before, but just the right shade of different. Although the album included Van's take on the old Cliff Richard, Nat King Cole, Tommy Edwards favourite 'It's All In The Game', this time critics didn't carp at the inclusion of a cover on a Van Morrison album. Six years on from 'Green', there were no longer suggestions that The Man's creative well had run dry.

'Into The Music' developed further the theme of a spiritual voyage which Morrison had embarked on during 'Veedon Fleece'. Cynics discerned a trend in rock'n'roll for religious regeneration – Bob Dylan had undergone a widely–publicised "born again" conversion to Christianity, and keenly shared his conversion with the proselytising 'Slow Train Coming' album. Looking back at the album, Van described himself to Steve Turner as "a Christian mystic... I'm not a Buddhist or a Hindu. I'm a Christian. I was born in a Christian environment in a Christian country". The specific religious references on 'Into The Music' are self evident: Morrison has himself "lifted up again" by the Lord; on 'Rolling Hills' the singer is to be found reading his Bible and living "his life in Him"...

'Bright Side Of The Road' was another irrepressibly jaunty album opener. Its opening line invokes the classic Dan Penn & Chips Moman soul ballad 'Dark End Of The Street', which everyone from Ry Cooder and Richard Thompson to James Carr had covered. 'Full Force Gale' is one of Morrison's most spare/honed and effective songs. Punchy and uplifting, its very economy lies at the heart of the song's greatness.

For all its buoyant melody and spiritual

optimism, 'Rolling Hills' featured one of Morrison's most mumbled and grumbled vocals on disc. It is the incongruity of Marcus' jaunty folkie violin and Morrison's gruff, tormented vocals which give the song its shape and distinctive quality. 'Stepping Out Queen' and 'You Make Me Feel So Free' were the fillers this time around, neither adding anything distinguished or fresh to Morrison's growing catalogue.

'Angeliou' is where Van really lets rip, "May" and "Paris" are the blue touchpapers which seem to get him going. The song is structured so that the search and journey lead into the next track 'And The Healing Has Begun'.

The subsequent two tracks, 'And The Healing Has Begun' and 'You Know What They're Writing About', were further manifestations of Van going deeper and deeper within himself. He seemed to be purging himself through the music, trying to attain wisdom by entering a trance-like state and exploring the healing power of music. He is wrestling with doubts and dilemmas, having a public dialogue with himself, and apparently gaining some sort of resolution (though certainly not a revelation) through these lengthy workouts, where time was no longer the point. It all went on as long as Van felt happy with it, and then it wound down, to silence.

Where is that mysterious plateau which Morrison reaches when he is so inspired? A dark and sombre place certainly, a cavern, perhaps ringing with Van's own idiosyncratic blend of Celtic R&B, Irish rock'n'roll, American jazz, blues and folk. When he gets properly into the groove, he spins off into another time and another place.

'And The Healing Has Begun' is no spiritual odyssey though. Morrison sings of a favourite Muddy Waters record, of returning from a gig, of rock'n'roll and making music with a violin and two guitars... It is a troubadour's testament to his muse, and to that other equally strong incentive which makes a young man follow the rock'n'roll route – what Morrison calls that "backstreet jellyroll".

Just as 'Santa Fe' segued seamlessly into 'Beautiful Obsession' on his previous album, Morrison pulls the same trick with 'It's All In The Game', which slips effortlessly into 'You Know What They're Writing About'.

This is Van roaring and ruminating. Like 'Listen To The Lion', 'You Know What They're Writing About' lets him meander in his own unique style. It's because it's Van Morrison, and because he is clearly on his way to somewhere else, that you allow him to get so worked up about a meeting "down by the pylons". Meetings in rock'n'roll take place up on the roof, under the board walk, or at the wrecking ball; you can meet on the corner or on the ledge... But by pylons?

VAN
MORRISON

COMMON
ONE

COMMON ONE

(POLYDOR 839 600-2, SEPTEMBER 1980)

If 'Into The Music' was a tentative public acknowledgement of Morrison's quest for spiritual values, 'Common One' was a veritable overdose of spiritual excesses.

'Common One' received some of the worst reviews of Morrison's whole career. Critics at the time were dismayed by The Man's determination to wear his spiritual influences so blatantly on his sleeve. Indeed there was precious little substance of any kind once you got past the clumsy name dropping and lush production.

The opening track 'Haunts Of Ancient Peace', is a reflective beginning. Van is shadowed by Mark Isham's distant trumpet as he walks the countryside, searching for Blake's new Jerusalem. Pee Wee Ellis' saxophone introduces a note of discord, but otherwise all is harmony. Surely the Holy Grail is only just around the corner?

'Satisfied', 'Wild Honey' and 'Spirit' all hover around the five minute mark, but are distinguished by neither melody nor lyric; indeed these three songs are fairly interchangeable with other sub-standard Morrison works from the preceding three years.

The album stands or falls by the two lengthy (15 minute) tracks, the ambitious 'Summertime In England', and 'When Heart Is Open' which drifts aimlessly over its sprawling and unfocused length. Whereas before Van could get away with engineering a meeting down by the pylons – and even inject a sense of purpose into the assignation – when he sings "Oh hand me down my big boots" on 'When Heart Is Open', even his staunchest supporters had difficulty keeping a straight face.

So that leaves 'Summertime In England', which actually isn't as bad as all that. Of course it's hopelessly self–indulgent, and it drops more names than the cover of *Hello!*, and it's as pretentious as a nouvelle cuisine menu.

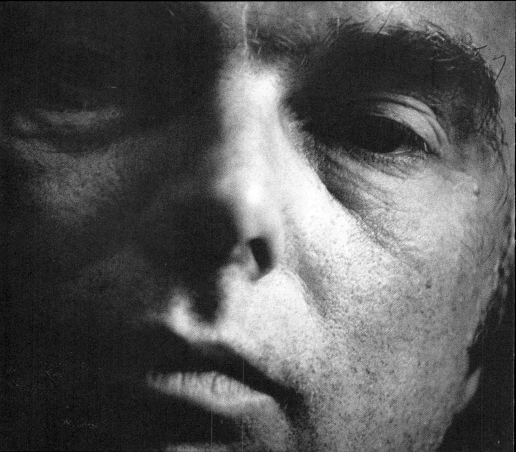

And yet, and yet...

At least Morrison doesn't hide his influences under a bushel, 'Summertime In England' brims over with name-checks. It's a cruise along the shelves of Van's library – Blake, Wordsworth, Eliot, Coleridge, Joyce, and just for good measure, Mahalia Jackson is in there too. "It ain't why" rages Van. "It just is!"

'Summertime In England' marks Morrison's first invocation of Avalon, a place which features prominently in Celtic mythology, and is popularly identified as the burial place of King Arthur. And the music... well it matches Van's word riffing. As he weaves the words, the drums of Peter Van Hooke propel the song. Electric bass and organ pepper the arrangement, but it's the accompanying strings which are used so memorably, as one big instrument, darting and piercing the song.

For years 'Summertime In England' was a stalwart of Morrison's increasingly confident live shows. Already 15 minutes on record, on stage the song would become a tin bucket into which Van could drop the latest names and influences.

"Self–indulgent" was the main criticism levelled at 'Common One'. Long–time admirers found the quality of the writing palpably weak as well. "'Did you ever hear about Wordsworth and Coleridge, baby?' must be one of his least inspired lines" wrote Steve Turner.

Johnny Rogan went even further: "On 'Common One'... Morrison... introduced some of the most embarrassing lyrics of his songwriting career. The album smacked of hip mysticism, gratuitous literary name-dropping, fourth form style poetry and repetitive scat-singing that was no longer effective but pointless and indulgent".

A change was now necessary. From 'Astral Weeks' to 'Veedon Fleece', Morrison had scarcely put a foot wrong. But after three years away and largely disappointing releases between 1977 and 1980, the old maestro urgently needed to turn over a new leaf.

VAN MORRISON
BEAUTIFUL VISION

BEAUTIFUL VISION
(POLYDOR 839 601-2, FEBRUARY 1982)

There was to be a gap of almost 18 months between 'Common One' and 'Beautiful Vision'. On holiday in San Francisco late in 1981, I couldn't believe that Van Morrison was playing just down the street. Checking the availability of tickets was literally along the lines of "What time does the show start?" – "What time can you get here?"

I wasn't expecting a whole helluva lot. My initial introduction to Van In Concert in 1979 had been one of the great rock'n'roll anticlimaxes of my life. 'Common One' had done little to restore my faith, and 'Beautiful Vision' was still four months away from release.

Working with a stripped down band, and playing a lot of keyboards, Morrison used the Palace Of Fine Arts gig as an opportunity to try out the unfamiliar 'Beautiful Vision' material. My first exposure to 'She Gives Me Religion' and 'Celtic Rain' were here, and Morrison was determined to give it all he'd got.

Even the sprawling 'Summertime In England' resonated. But it was the new songs from 'Beautiful Vision' which offered up hope. I recall Van encoring with 'Buona Sera' – a surprise move this – an age-old hit for Louis Prima and Acker Bilk, Emil Ford & The Checkmates had taken the song into the rock'n'roll era in the UK. From that same pre-Beatle era, Van encored with Johnny Kidd & The Pirates' throbbing 'Shakin' All Over' – arguably the most authentic slab of British rock'n'roll ever. In keeping with the party spirit he was engendering from the stage, Van asked if anyone out there remembered Cliff Richard? The Britpop constituency, we happy few, whooped our remembrance, and Van slid into a spritely 'Gloria', which he dedicated to Cliff.

On its release early in 1982, 'Beautiful Vision' invigorated Morrison's standing, which was further buoyed by a four night stint at London's Dominion

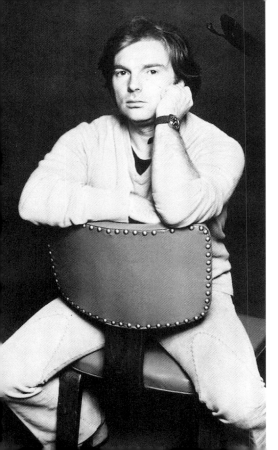

Theatre, just by Centre Point in the centre of London. Those Dominion shows blew away any unhappy memories of Van Morrison In Concert, and reminded those lucky enough to have witnessed them, of his triumphant Rainbow shows a decade before.

The re-awakening of interest, and re-acceptance of Van Morrison as a major player on the Eighties rock scene, had a lot to do with the success of 'Beautiful Vision'. At 37 Morrison cut an incongruous figure amidst the pretty-boy, peacock finery of Duran Duran and Spandau Ballet, but his musical credibility and unwillingness to stay in one place ensured his acceptance by succeeding generations. Like Neil Young, Bruce Springsteen and Bob Dylan, it was Morrison's integrity of purpose which appealed to hard-core music lovers. For all his truculence in interview, see-saw concert performances and sporadically brilliant albums, Van Morrison was obviously no tool of the increasingly homogenised rock'n'roll industry. Van went his own sweet way,

and occasionally that wayward journey coincided with popular taste.

Van has never been a mainstream act, and he will not cause the likes of Phil Collins or George Michael sleepless nights with his relatively humble sales figures. But his records have sold consistently and steadily over the years, and every time there's an appraisal of "The Greatest Albums Ever Made", 'Astral Weeks' is almost certain to be there, often with a sprinkling of other Van favourites.

Following the mixed reception accorded 'A Period Of Transition', 'Wavelength' and 'Common One', it had looked like Van was creatively on the ropes, then along came 'Beautiful Vision'. While it wasn't anything like as seamless as any one of his first three striking albums, 'Beautiful Vision' demonstrated Morrison's ability to combine creativity with personal spiritual questing, and it proved a most satisfactory combination.

'Celtic Ray' was a muted opening, but soon developed into a clarion call to "Ireland, Scotland, England, Wales..." Van is keening to go home: "I've been away too long". After a decade living in America, Morrison had relocated full-time to England, finally settling near Ladbroke Grove, the Bohemian area of West London which he had mentioned on 'Astral Weeks'. It was the same territory which had infused the stark 'TB Sheets' all those years before.

Morrison's reconciliation of his muse and his inspiration coincided with a similar state of mind for Bob Dylan; after two albums of born–again material, Dylan's 1981 'Shot Of Love' reaffirmed his position as rock's pre-eminent songwriter. Morrison has even gone on record with his admiration for Dylan – "Dylan is the greatest living poet" he unambiguously told Bill Flanagan.

'Northern Muse (Solid Ground)' was a further rumination on religion, which paid homage to Dylan with its references to 'If You See Her, Say Hello', from another of Bob's many comeback albums, 1974's 'Blood On The Tracks'. Van sings of the "solid ground of the

County Down", and the Irish elements of the song were enhanced by Sean Folsom's uileann pipes. It was not to be the only reference to his Irish background on 'Beautiful Vision'.

The pounding 'Dweller On The Threshold' is one of Morrison's most convincing depictions of his frequent quests for spiritual enlightenment. It is a journey from the darkness into light, and propelled by Tom Dollinger's relentless drum and cymbal rhythm, Van takes you along for the ride. The song was co-written with engineer Hugh Murphy, who had been a partner of Gerry Rafferty's, and worked with the Scottish singer-songwriter on the 1979 smash 'Baker Street'. Murphy also helped Morrison out on two further songs for 'Beautiful Vision' – 'Aryan Mist' and 'Across The Bridge Where Angels Dwell'.

If the title track allowed standards to dip, Van was back on course with 'She Gives Me Religion'. The song features one of Van's welcome lion-roaring vocals, as well as a chorus of powerful sincerity.

'Cleaning Windows' is a delightful and

clear segment of autobiography. A snap-shot of the young George Ivan growing up in Belfast, remembering the smell of the bakery across the road, blowing saxophone on Saturday nights and enjoying his schoolboy job cleaning windows – "No.36" shouts Van at one point, presumably recalling the site of a particularly successful window clean. The track also contains the most comprehensive shopping list of any Van song apart from 'Summertime In England', namechecking the "singing brakeman" Jimmie Rodgers, Leadbelly, Blind Lemon Jefferson, Sonny Terry & Brownie McGhee, Muddy Waters, Zen judge Christmas Humphreys and Jack Kerouac. Steve Turner notes that Morrison was dating a Danish girl around the time of recording 'Beautiful Vision'. She from the Vanlose district of Copenhagen, so no mere coincidence that the next song on the album was 'Vanlose Stairway', in which aside from a trunk load of religious tomes, Van also asks to be sent some loving and some kissing. Presumably the brooding instrumental

'Scandinavia' which closes the album had its source in the same relationship.

'Aryan Mist' and 'Scandinavia' add little to the whole, but the penultimate track 'Across The Bridge Where Angels Dwell' pounds along with the fervour of 'Dweller On The Threshold'. Van's vocal suggesting frailty and uncertainty, not the blustering confidence of yore. Allegedly written about his daughter Shana, the song is one of the most sensitive and fragile in Morrison's whole career.

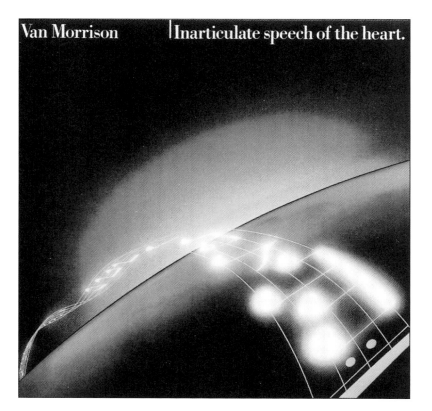

INARTICULATE SPEECH OF THE HEART

(POLYDOR 839 604–2, MARCH 1983)

The clue was to be found at the bottom of the back sleeve of Morrison's 13th album: "Special thanks: L. Ron Hubbard". Hubbard was the controversial author and founder of the Church of Scientology, who first came to fame in 1950 with his book Dianetics, which became the basis of the Scientology cult. Growing concerns over the methods of Scientology saw Hubbard banned from entering Britain in 1968.

The Scientology HQ in Britain was on Tottenham Court Road in London, coincidentally only a few yards from the Dominion Theatre, which Morrison continued to use as his base for concerts in the capital. Reports in 1983 during his six night spell at the venue to promote 'Inarticulate Speech Of The Heart', had Morrison handing out Scientology literature to the audience queuing to get into his show.

Reluctant to discuss his ongoing quest, Morrison did admit that he had undergone Scientology auditing, but the general impression given was that while Scientology did interest him, so did Christianity, Buddhism, Rosicrucianism and a whole bunch of other religions.

'Inarticulate Speech Of The Heart' is a workmanlike Van Morrison album, but while clearly cut from the same template as 'Beautiful Vision', it lacks its predecessor's passion and freshness. Four of the album's 11 songs are instrumentals, no bad thing in the case of the gentle, rural atmospherics of 'Connswater' or the sweeping landscape of 'Inarticulate Speech Of The Heart No.1', but decidedly stretched over the lacklustre elevator moods of 'Celtic Swing' and 'September Night'.

'The Street Only Knew Your Name' swings along amiably enough without causing too much excitement, until Van cranks it up a gear near three minutes in. Suddenly we're back in 'Cleaning Windows' territory, as Van spells out his favourite Gene Vincent songs: 'Be

Bop A Lula', 'Who Slapped John', 'Boppin' The Blues' and 'You Make Me Feel Alright'.

'Higher Than the World' and 'Inarticulate Speech Of The Heart No.2' are both satisfactory enough, but they lack the pounding heart which infused the best of Morrison's work during the Eighties. 'River Of Time' has a sinewy chorus which stays with you, and the song's atmospherics are well in keeping with the mood which Morrison strives to convey elsewhere on the album. However the title of 'Irish Heartbeat' offers more than the song delivers.

While far from being an essential addition to the catalogue, 'Inarticulate Speech Of The Heart' is saved from being straight down the dumper material by at least two tracks – 'Rave On John Donne' and 'Cry For Home'.

'Rave On John Donne' was to jostle for position with 'Summertime In England' as the Morrison litany song in live shows of the period. Apart from being one of the all-time great rock'n'roll song titles, who besides Van could unite the spirit of

Buddy Holly and the great 17th Century metaphysical poet in the same breath? Only Morrison had the balls to be so explicitly pretentious. 'Rave On John Donne' was a season ticket into Van's library. It showed you where he had been, and where he was going: Walt Whitman, Omar Khayam, Kahlil Gibran, and lest we forget, "rave on Mr Yeats!"

Despite the bargain-basement poetry, philosophy, nature and theosophy, this is the sort of song which hurls Morrison into the vanguard. In anyone else's hands it would be preposterous, and even in Van's hands it teeters on the brink; but there is something in that urgent Irish/American voice begging, pleading, cajoling and ordering his cast of characters into action, which simply cannot be ignored.

It is Morrison's ability to make the words rave on the printed page as well as in your heart. It is the audacity and boldness of his epiphany that moves and touches. In this song – which manages to be both farcical and somehow strangely affecting – you find yourself warming to Van Morrison and his unashamed, naïve

hymn of devotion to those who have inspired him.

The other side of the coin was the taut and rock'n'roll friendly 'Cry For Home'. Following the self indulgence of 'Rave On John Donne', 'Cry For Home' displayed the disciplined pop star side of Van Morrison. Much as he might dislike being reminded of it from the vantage point of his maturity, back in the Sixties, both with Them under the tutelage of Bert Berns and on his own 'Moondance' and 'His Band And The Street Choir' albums, Morrison had proved adept at producing perfect three minute slices of radio bliss. 'Cry For Home' was another one to add to an impressive list which already included 'Gloria', 'Brown Eyed Girl' and 'Domino'.

Many of the elements which had made 'Into The Mystic' so moving are found again on 'Cry For Home'. Van's vulnerable vocal, the palpable, aching desire to quit the distant shores and make for the safe harbour of home, seem real. Like Van, you know that "when you hear the call..."

A SENSE OF WONDER
(POLYDOR 843 116–2, FEBRUARY 1985)

Well strike me pink, if that ain't the old curmudgeon on the front sleeve – smiling! And is that really Van on the back too, modelling what can only be described as "Zorro chic"? And stap me vitals, is this the first authenticated Van Morrison sleeve note concerning the exploits of Boffyflow & Spike?

'A Sense Of Wonder' effectively concludes the trilogy begun with 'Beautiful Vision' and 'Inarticulate Speech Of The Heart' which carried Morrison through the first half of the Eighties. These three records were Van's voyages; The Man setting off in search of just what made him, us, the universe, tick. He had of course tried it all before – 'Common One' in 1980 had been a quantum leap – but he only began to reconcile the quest with his music, on the 'Beautiful Vision' album. For the time being 'A Sense Of Wonder' was a satisfactory conclusion.

Much of the music on the album reflected Morrison's involvement with an organisation called The Wrekin Trust, established in 1971 to "awaken the vision of the spiritual nature of man and the universe, and to help people to develop themselves as vehicles for channelling spiritual energies into society".

Morrison's interest in The Wrekin Trust came as a result of their shared belief in the healing power of music, and the marriage between the music and the spirit. In 1987 Morrison and the Trust presented a conference, The Secret Heart Of Music, which was described as "an exploration into the power of music to change consciousness". In the pamphlet which accompanied the conference, Van's self–penned biographical profile came close to expounding his own musical philosophy: "His passion for music and his bemusement with the contradictions inherent in being famous have led him to deeply question many of the underlying attitudes of our age... His own work is now increasingly intended as a means for inducing contemplation and for healing and uplifting the soul... "His struggle to reconcile the mythic, almost otherworldly vision of the Celts and his own search for spiritual satisfaction, with the apparent hedonism of blues and soul music, has produced many inspired and visionary performances."

Such a statement throws up some interesting points. Morrison's statement that his music was "increasingly intended as a means for inducing contemplation and for healing and uplifting the soul.." would come as news to a number of journalists whom Morrison had virtually reduced to tears with displays of arrogant truculence and wilful non-communication. The statement would also raise the odd eyebrow among audiences who had sat through perversely selfish performances while Morrison arrogantly strutted his stuff.

Mercifully, little of Morrison's bile and spite was apparent on 'A Sense Of Wonder'; instead, there was a sense of light-heartedness and almost spritely

joie de vivre. The music was as sombre and introspective as you would expect from the Van of that period, but 'A Sense Of Wonder' successfully managed to balance the earnest questing with Morrison's uplifting musical genius.

The opening track 'Tore Down A La Rimbaud' was another piledriving sleight of hand (a la 'Rave On John Donne'), of the kind only Morrison was capable of pulling off. Arthur Rimbaud was a French Symbolist poet who first published, to great acclaim, while still a teenager during the Seventies. However following the poor reviews accorded his *A Season In Hell,* he gave up writing at the tender age of 19. The remainder of his life was spent in dissolute travel until, barely into his Thirties, he died penniless. Rimbaud had influenced Bob Dylan during the mid–Sixties, but quite what Van got from him is hardly apparent from this song; nonetheless it acts as a striking beginning to a remarkable record.

Even the instrumentals – 'Evening Meditation' and 'Boffyflow & Spike' –

are marked improvements upon the undistinguished lyric-free pieces which peppered 'Inarticulate Speech Of The Heart'. The musical liveliness undoubtedly having much to do with the presence of the fiery, Irish folk-rock ensemble Moving Hearts.

'Ancient Of Days', 'The Master's Eyes' and 'A New Kind Of Man' are further testaments to Van's pursuit of the unknowable. Not content with demonstrating his cleverness at being able to convey such wide–ranging issues in his own songs, he even translates a Ray Charles song 'What Would I Do', into a pensive, meditative rumination upon existence and faith. The album's other cover is a breezy take on Mose Allison's 'If You Only Knew'.

'Let The Slave' is Van's version of a William Blake poem, arranged by poet Adrian Mitchell and jazz musician Mike Westbrook. Morrison's interest in Blake is well documented, but for all the poet's interest in mysticism and divinity he was also a social commentator, and 'Let The Slave' combines both aspects of the man.

'A Sense Of Wonder' is, of course, further testament to Van's belief in the existence of a higher power; but alongside his preoccupation with the "eternal presence" and "fiery visions", the song also documents Morrison's fascination with eating. He concludes with a spoken recitation, in that compelling and quietly unique Celtic-American burr, listing a litany of half–remembered meals and childhood snacks: pastie suppers, Wagon Wheels, snowballs... Van Morrison & His Tummy is a subject to which we shall return.

NO GURU, NO METHOD, NO TEACHER

(POLYDOR 849 619-2, JULY 1986)

If 'A Sense Of Wonder' had confirmed Van's spirituality and his relentless pursuit of something which just exceeded his grasp, with influences ranging from William Blake to Mose Allison and music coming atcha from Moving Hearts and Ray Charles; then 'No Guru, No Method, No Teacher' was Van back on the beat. The album was musically stripped down, leaving a core band which allowed Morrison ample opportunity to roam.

Fifteen albums into his career, Van showed no sign of flagging with the cumbersomely titled, though musically uplifting, 'No Guru, No Method, No Teacher'. Indeed there is a consistency to the album which recalls much of Morrison's best work from the Seventies. For while it displayed Morrison still determined to pursue the lodestar of his own spiritual odyssey, this was also an album of Van reflecting where he had come from.

'Got To Go Back' begins with the young Van, back in East Belfast's Orangefield, listening to Ray Charles. This is 'Cleaning Windows' with knobs on: Van pining for his Irish homeland, missing his stout, aware that any Irish song will make him cry. He has to go back to the land which bred him.

'Oh The Warm Feeling' and 'Foreign Window' follow, devotional songs which you could perm into any number of preceding Van Morrison albums.

Where 'No Guru, No Method, No Teacher' really kicks in though, is with the scathing 'A Town Called Paradise', outstanding because instead of going all gooey and meditational and contemplative, here Van sounds positively venomous. Beginning with a weaving riff which recalls 'Astral Weeks', Van leaves you in little doubt just where he's coming from as he growls: "Copycats ripped off my songs". 'A Town Called Paradise' is vintage Van, Morrison riffing on a mood, buoyed by bass and bolstered by brass. He knows that Paradise is empty unless it's shared, and he sweeps along on the wave of the song to get there, together.

Van had copycats on his mind. In 1985 he said in an interview: "For years, people have been saying to me – you know, nudge, nudge – have you heard this guy Springsteen? You should really check him out. I just ignored it. Then four or five months ago, I was in Amsterdam and a friend of mine put on a video. Springsteen came on the video and that was the first time I ever saw him, and he's definitely ripped me off. There's no doubt about that. Not only did Springsteen... I mean, he's even ripped off my movements as well. My Seventies movements, you know what I mean?" Even by Van's standards, this is an extraordinary statement: odd enough that he hadn't seen Springsteen until a good 12 years after his début album, but the idea that Bruce Springsteen – who even detractors must concede is one of rock's most athletic stars – would rip off Van Morrison's

"movements" causes the mind to bend, stretch, and frankly boggle.

'In The Garden' had already been used as a title, for one of the outstanding tracks on Bob Dylan's 1980 born-again album 'Saved', and Van's 'In The Garden' was cut from similarly inspirational cloth. Beautifully setting the scene in a garden after a summer shower, Van rolls on through further pastoral bliss, nodding toward Blake and his image of "infinity in a flower". By verse six, he invokes the spirit of 'Madame George' (the trance, the "childlike vision") before admitting to being born again and feeling "the presence of the Christ".

It's unclear whether the girl to whom the song is addressed is a spirit herself, or the inspiration, but Morrison is soon making it apparent that he needs no one else. He doesn't need a guru, a method or a teacher. What is without cannot be forgotten, but the truth is within.

As well as being the name of a dodgy Irish folk act of the Seventies, 'Tir Na Nog' is one of the many Celtic names for Eire. It is also the title of another of the songs on 'No Guru, No Method, No Teacher' which suggest Morrison's return to his Irish roots. Jeff Labes' strings shadow Morrison's prowling vocal, while the background of rain, mountains, the sun in the West, the Church of Ireland and cool streams, all point to Van's rediscovery of his Celtic heritage.

That elemental, mystic, Gaelic aspect is further emphasised by the unambiguous 'One Irish Rover', while the main point of interest in 'Here Comes The Knight' is Morrison's impish retitling of his best–loved Them song (Bert Berns' 'Here Comes The Night') to embrace the era of "knights in armour talking chivalry".

'Thanks For The Information' is, amongst other things, a wilful recycling of cliches ("never give a sucker an even break", "a bird in the hand is worth two in the bush", "two steps forwards, three steps back"...). Interpreting a Van Morrison lyric is only slightly less hazardous than attempting to dissect a Dylan song; and this is as inscrutable as any major song in the catalogue. Maybe Van's complaining about modern information overload or, more likely, he's saying that although you might think you can get all the advice you want, ultimately you just have to carry on on your own.

'No Guru, No Method, No Teacher' wraps with 'Ivory Tower', another of those taut and lean, three minute Van Morrison R&B workouts, with a guitar figure which, to these ears, is reminiscent of 'Here Comes The Night'.

Van played Dublin's Self Aid prior to the album's release. Hot on the heels of the preceding summer's Live Aid, Van appeared alongside U2, The Pogues, The Boomtown Rats and Elvis Costello. Evidently warming to the event, Morrison took to the stage, from whence he proclaimed: "If I was a gunslinger, there'd be a lot of dead copycats around" before launching into a vicious 'A Town Called Paradise'.

For all his search for inner calm and endless reading of texts designed to

induce serenity and contemplation,
there obviously remained a secular side
to Van which just wouldn't lie down.

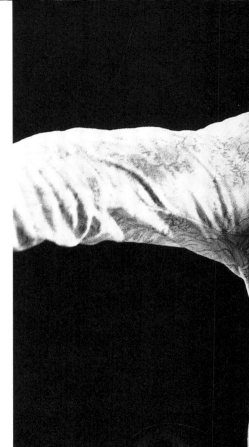

Van Morrison · Poetic Champions Compose

POETIC CHAMPIONS COMPOSE

(POLYDOR 517 217–2, SEPTEMBER 1987)

After a stunning run of albums throughout the decade, Van ground to a halt. 'Poetic Champions Compose' is a workmanlike Van Morrison album, but after the heights scaled on 'No Guru, No Method, No Teacher', there was little to really excite or inspire here.

Still closely involved with The Wrekin Trust, Morrison was now using music as an open forum to debate the nature of his own spirituality. While this questing was apparent on 'No Guru, No Method, No Teacher', that album also dealt with Van's parallel desire to return to his Irish roots. On 'Poetic Champions Compose', the journey was restricted to simply looking inside himself.

The problem many fans had with Van's work, was the same dilemma Dylan fans faced when Bob was "born again". Rock'n'roll is actually a very conservative form: rock stars can go out and preach on behalf of free love, boast of their prodigious drug intake, proselytise about their fondness for firearms... but as soon as they dare to start talking about religion, it's drift

away time. No one denied Morrison his right to search, indeed his journeys often made him a more exhilarating musical companion, but by the time of 'Poetic Champions Compose', there was a widespread feeling that we had all been down this well–trodden road just a few too many times before.

The album's outstanding track was 'Queen Of The Slipstream', a line from which provided the album with its title. Part of its appeal lay in the delicately plucked harp, which added an extra texture to Van's mysterious voyage. This was one of those tracks where Van grooved into his own world, and you were happy simply to cling to his coat-tails. The song gave him the opportunity to spread and roam, and a sense of freedom that was missing from tracks such as 'The Mystery'.

The jaunty 'Give Me My Rapture' achieved that same devotional and inspirational spirit, while the sense of mystery was recaptured on the wilfully obscure 'Alan Watts Blues'. The latter track has a light, almost skittish melody, and – as he sings "I'm cloud hidden… whereabouts unknown" – one of Van's most driven lyrics.

The three instrumentals, 'Spanish Steps', 'Celtic Excavation' and 'Allow Me', allow Van ample opportunity to range on his alto saxophone; while the vocal tracks 'I Forgot That Love Existed' and 'Someone Like You', present Van on automatic pilot. 'Did Ye Get Healed' was to become a staple of live sets, allowing Morrison the opportunity to roam. Asking the question in concert, he would whip himself up into a lather, possessed by a fierce determination to know the answer, whereas here on record, he sounds merely curious.

'Sometimes I Feel Like A Motherless Child' was Van's reworking of the old Negro spiritual, which had previously seen service in the hands of Paul

Robeson, Marian Anderson and Fats Waller. Van's version was brooding and sombre, the song's sentiments fitting in perfectly with his own quest – for personal liberation allied to spiritual enlightenment.

It is strange that Morrison has so rarely felt like tackling spirituals, because he is one of the few white men who can convincingly approximate the gruff, painful quality of vocal improvisation to be found in the best interpreters of black music. On 'Sometimes I Feel Like A Motherless Child', it is Van's spectral reading of the song which gives it its edge. The light percussion somehow further darkens the mood, and Van avoids vocal histrionics, letting the centuries-old sentiments build and grow.

As a vocalist, Van loses himself in the song. In concert, he uses the material simply as a springboard to leap into the mystic. He is quite capable of losing himself, and finding the quality with which the best black singers of whatever genre – blues, soul, R&B or gospel – display their virtuosity and genius.

'Poetic Champions Compose' is hardly an essential Van Morrison album, but it allowed yer man further opportunities to delve and dive in his search for God. That search had long been Morrison's preoccupation, and as his former personal assistant Chris Hodgkin told Steve Turner: "He tended to align himself with Christianity, but he was also into pre-Christian things. I would say that he was more interested in the Western mystical tradition. He was a pretty weird Christian".

IRISH HEARTBEAT

VAN MORRISON & THE CHIEFTAINS

IRISH HEARTBEAT

(MERCURY 834 496–2, JUNE 1988)

A marriage made, if not in Heaven, then at least in Belfast, had Van tying up with Ireland's most successful musical export after U2. The Chieftains had been famous for their inspired interpretations of traditional Irish music since they first formed in 1963, though it took the group a full decade to give up their day jobs.

Jo Lustig, the pre–eminent "folk" manager during the Seventies, who had managed Steeleye Span, Richard & Linda Thompson and Ralph McTell, booked the group into the Royal Albert Hall on St Patrick's Night 1975, a move which elevated them onto the world platform, and they had never looked back.

Under the inspired musical leadership of Paddy Moloney, The Chieftains went from strength to strength – scoring Stanley Kubrick's lavish period drama *Barry Lyndon*, and supplying musical muscle to albums as varied as those by Mick Jagger, Art Garfunkel and Glenn Frey. But by 1988, The Chieftains' musical standing was dipping. They were seen as undiscriminating guns for hire, traditional musicians who had sold their souls for commercial success.

Van Morrison could not help but be aware of The Chieftains. The only surprise about 'Irish Heartbeat' was that it had taken them so long to get together. Following an Irish TV appearance together, on St Patrick's Day 1988, Van and The Chieftains undertook a UK tour, which garnered both acts the best recent reviews of their careers.

The music of The Chieftains could barely be bettered, whether on rollicking jigs and reels, or heart–tugging ballads and airs. On stage with them, Van loosened up considerably, cracking jokes and clearly enjoying the camaraderie. Maybe because it was music with which he had been familiar since his youth, maybe because it took the pressure off him to be the serious and intense "Van Morrison" of legend... whatever the reason, those Morrison shows with The Chieftains were among the highlights of his concert career.

An album together was the next logical step, and 'Irish Heartbeat' did little to disappoint. As well as bringing Van and The Chieftains together, the album included special guests Mary Black and De Dannan's Maura O'Connell.

The 'Irish Heartbeat' only grows weak when The Man decides to go back to being "Van Morrison" again. 'Raglan Road' and 'My Lagan Love' are immeasurably diminished by Morrison's growling "soulful" interpretations. What works so well on his own material, often sending him off into some sort of musical reverie, is incongruous and faintly risible here. The vocal affectations of rock'n'roll, soul and R&B seem wilfully at odds with the traditional Irish music. If you didn't know him any better, you'd swear it was Morrison's attempt to upstage The Chieftains and claim the 'Irish Heartbeat' package as his own.

Before 'Irish Heartbeat', these songs had been very much the province of familiar Irish singers from the early days of sound recording like John McCormack, or easy listening favourites such as Foster & Allen or Daniel O'Donnell. In company with The Chieftains, Morrison brought the songs to a whole new audience.

It was an appropriate time to be unearthing the folk music which had played such a formative role in his musical education. By the end of the Eighties, 'Unplugged' (the trendy name for folk-influenced music) was all the vogue. Kevin Rowland and Dexy's Midnight Runners had quit the scene, taking their idiosyncratic brand of Celtic soul with them, but bands such as The Pogues, The Men They Couldn't Hang and The Boot Hill Foot Tappers were not ashamed to admit the influence of The Dubliners on their own music. While upcoming acts such as The Proclaimers, Everything But The Girl and The Bangles were happy to reveal that their influences came as much from Nick Drake and Fairport Convention as from rock'n'roll.

'Irish Heartbeat' tapped into the

reawakened interest in indigenous music; but it was no calculated commercial enterprise, for better (usually) or for worse, Van Morrison has always gone his own way.

The irrepressible 'I'll Tell Me Ma' had been recorded by The Dubliners and The Clancy Brothers, and was a song Morrison had particularly fond memories of as a child growing up in Belfast. 'Marie's Wedding' was a Scottish favourite which Billy Connolly loved to play on the banjo. It had been popularised by accordion king Jimmy Shand (himself made legendary by Richard Thompson's 'Don't Step On My Jimmy Shands') and was a staple in the repertoire of Scots marching bands and bagpipe ensembles.

'She Moves Through The Fair' had seen service in the hands of every major Irish singer – John McCormack, Margaret Barry, The McPeake Family – and was then taken up by innumerable other folk music fans, including Fairport Convention, Art Garfunkel, Barbara Dickson, Feargal Sharkey, Marianne Faithfull and Mike Oldfield.

Of all the songs on 'Irish Heartbeat', 'Carrickfergus' is perhaps the best-loved. One of the most haunting airs ever composed, the song has long been recognised for its own inimitable qualities, and over the years has been covered by Joan Baez, Bryan Ferry and The Cowboy Junkies, as well as every Irish act of note.

Leaving aside Van's occasional incongruous vocal mannerisms, 'Irish Heartbeat' is a triumphant return to form for all parties. Even the two Morrison originals ('Irish Heartbeat' and 'Celtic Ray') are marked improvements on the original versions featured respectively on 'Inarticulate Speech Of The Heart' and 'Beautiful Vision'.

It's a joy to hear Morrison let rip on 'Star Of The County Down' and 'I'll Tell Me Ma', or go all gooily meditative on 'Carrickfergus' and 'She Moved Through The Fair', and it's also worth a chuckle to hear Van of all people sing "Step we gaily as we go," as if he really means it on 'Marie's Wedding'. He is in

good company too, The Chieftains' backing is with him every step of the way. On their recent star-studded albums, The Chieftains have too often appeared as guests at their own feast, but here the sympatico with Morrison is self evident, and the blend of bodhran, fiddles and Paddy Moloney's uilleann pipes behind Van is as sublime a collaboration as you are likely to get on disc.

Morrison and The Chieftains' Paddy Moloney belatedly undertook some interviews to promote the project. *NME*'s long-suffering Gavin Martin irked Van straight-off when he was impertinent enough to ask if the combination of the two guaranteed sales… "Well, if you have all the answers, you tell me. I'll just sit here and listen, it will save me work." Later, Van called the album: "Basically a cross-section of Irish music, from stage Irish to deep roots going back to traditional Irish and back to new age Irish to Celtic revival to street songs. It was trying to get some sense of unity."

Morrison's search for a spiritual har-

bour was a voyage of turbulence and constant questing; Cliff's Christianity was well established and content. Cliff had become a public Christian at a time when his pre-eminent position as Britain's top pop star was challenged only by The Beatles. These beliefs became front page news when he testified at a Billy Graham meeting in London in 1966. Cliff's very public Christianity seemed to emphasise the 26 year-old's squareness in a rock'n'roll scene busy coming to terms with The Rolling Stones, The Who and The Beatles' experimentation on 'Revolver', and his image had remained the same ever since.

AVALON SUNSET

(POLYDOR 839 262-2, JUNE 1989)

On a roll following his collaboration with The Chieftains (which was reprised when Morrison appeared as a special guest on The Chieftains 1989 album, 'A Celebration', performing 'Boffyflow & Spike'), and with his credibility intact on into the Eighties, Van Morrison wrong-footed everyone when the opening track of his 18th solo album boasted a duet with clean-living Christian, Cliff Richard.

Morrison had met Cliff at a Christian arts group party, and wrote 'Whenever God Shines His Light', which would give him only his second Top 20 hit in the UK, with Cliff in mind. "I grew up with Cliff" Van told *NME*. "He'd be on Saturday Club. I was a teenager you know..."

'Avalon Sunset' saw another familiar name from Van's rock'n'roll past make his debut on a Morrison album. Georgie Fame who is here credited with Hammond organ is best remembered for his Sixties pop hits 'Yeh Yeh', 'Get Away' and 'The Ballad Of Bonnie & Clyde', although he was also recognised as one the best R&B singers of the time. His career since disbanding The Blue Flames had erred more towards jazz, and when he made his début with Morrison on 'Avalon Sunset', it marked the beginning of a musical collaboration which still continues today.

Nominally to promote the album, Van agreed to be interviewed for *Q* by one of his few living idols, comedian Spike Milligan, who he had already immortalised on 'Boffyflow & Spike'. Van had fond memories of Milligan's comic genius from *The Goon Show*. "He was just always there," he reminisced to *Q*'s Paul Du Noyer. "Sunday mornings, if I remember, was *The Goons*... (they) were huge in Ireland; kids I grew up with talked like that all the time."

When pressed by Milligan on his personal life, Morrison responded: "I'm not used to this just talking about anything. I'm not into talking about myself with journalists. I talk about the music. The fact is that I do this for a living, and then I have my own life which is separate from that. So Van Morrison makes records, and I'm separate from that. That's just what I do for a job... I can't mix my personal stuff with the job, so I just talk about my job. I'm not interested in selling myself, I just sell my records, my music. So I have to censor everything I say, 'cos if I don't, they just use it against me..."

Spike himself was interviewed by *Q* in 1996, but he had no fond memories of his 1989 encounter with Morrison: "The man was a pig... looked dirty and scruffy, though it might be an act. I said 'How are you?' 'Are you married?' – just small talk – and he said to me 'I didn't come to talk about all that crap, I want to talk about my new record...' Then he left the room and went outside, and he'd spilt coffee all over the floor. So I

took all my clothes off and I put on a big black hat and my false nose – the penis nose – and he laughed. I thought 'fucking hell, you have to do a lot to make him laugh!'"

'Avalon Sunset' had all the muscle and variety necessary to cement it as a great Van Morrison album. The title reflected Morrison's continued interest in the mystic quest for the Avalon of pre-history and the album itself further expounded Morrison's quest for spiritual satisfaction.

'Whenever God Shines His Light' was the most manifest example of Morrison's Christian commitment. The fact that he shared the vocal with Britain's best–known Christian entertainer, together with the emphatically Christian lyrics, left little doubt as to Morrison's devotion. The song was lifted off as a single, and gave Morrison his highest UK chart placing since his days with Them over 20 years before. 'Whenever God Shines His Light' is not one of Morrison's most outstanding songs, but as a testament of faith, it fulfils its purpose.

A far better exploration occurs on 'When Will I Ever Learn To Live With God'. Stripped of Cliff's chipper vocals, the song centres on a still questing Van and makes for far more dramatic listening than the easy certainties of the earlier track. 'When Will I Ever Learn To Live With God' finds the majesty of the deity in the green countryside, in the glow of evening, the shepherd and his sheep and the art and architecture of the centuries.

To *NME* at the time, Morrison admitted his spiritual odysseys: "I'm into all of it, orthodox or otherwise. I don't accept or reject any of it. I'm not searching for anything in particular. I'm just groping in the dark... for a bit more light".

'Contacting My Angel' is perfunctory, and the ominously titled 'I'd Love To Write Another Song' is a loose, jazz swing which finds Van "searching for inspiration" so he can write something which will "pay the bills". By coincidence, the following track of 'Avalon Sunset' did just that.

'Have I Told You Lately' remains one of Morrison's best-known songs, largely thanks to Rod Stewart's cover which reached No 5 in the UK in 1993. However, a certain amount of confusion ensued with an earlier song, Scott Wiseman's 'Have I Told You Lately That I Love You?', which since being recorded by Bing Crosby in 1945, had become a ballad standard covered by hundreds of singers, including Elvis Presley, Tony Bennett, Willie Nelson, Jim Reeves and Slim Whitman.

Van's 'Have I Told You Lately' has the old chuckler in a mood not that far removed from slushily sentimental. Lushly orchestrated, the song is tranquil and unashamedly sloppy. Following on from a song bemoaning his lack of inspiration, 'Have I Told You Lately' sounds almost like Morrison proving he can, when necessary, turn his hand to writing a straight-no-chaser ballad. The song, with a less sentimental reading from the composer, reunited Morrison with The Chieftains on their 'Long Black Veil' album of 1995, a version which benefits from a poignant harp and flute intro.

From here on in, 'Avalon Sunset' builds into a classic addition to Morrison's catalogue: 'Coney Island' has the great man evoking memories of childhood holidays around Lillough and Ardglass, the beautiful border territory of Downpatrick. It's also another of those Van songs which list snacks with mouth-watering relish, in this case mussels and potted herrings ("in case we get famished before dinner"). *Q* magazine once listed 10 songs concerning themselves with "enticing comestibles painstakingly detailed on Van Morrison records", from "You're the apple of my eye/The ice cream in my cherry pie" from 1967's 'Ro Ro Rosey' to the sea food lovingly listed on 'Coney Island'.

When I was there a couple of years ago, Coney Island itself – like Cyprus Avenue, the Graceland of Morrison iconography – didn't seem like a rock'n'roll landmark. It's just a low-lying spit of land with holiday cottages, hardly an island at all. But when Morrison sings of the place, it's obviously magic, a

place where "the crack was good", and in closing there is that sense of wonder in his voice as he asks "wouldn't it be great if it was like this all the time?". Coney Island obviously meant a lot to Van way back then.

'I'm Tired Joey Boy' has all the hallmarks of a traditional song which Morrison learnt by osmosis. But it is down as an original Van Morrison composition, and it's also down as one of his best. Economical and heartfelt, but for all its familiar quest for rural simplicity, a very un-Morrison song.

"Conservatism bring you to boredom" and "I've no time for schism…" aren't lines that flow happily, but Van makes something truly timeless of the line "Oh I'm tired Joey boy of the makings of men". A little nugget.

'Orangefield' sprang from the sort of "Ulster day" Van sings of in the song's final verse. In 1956, the 11 year-old George Ivan Morrison began attending Orangefield Boys' School near his childhood home. A lifetime later, Van sprinkles the Belfast district with a sense of wonder as he sings of eternal true love, now, and then in those dappled autumn days in Orangefield.

'Daring Night' is another frequently overlooked gem in the Cartier cluster which is Morrison's back catalogue: Van takes the song by the throat and just won't let go. Inexplicably never released as a single, the song piledrives its way into your memory, while a beautiful tension is sustained between Arty McGlynn's acoustic guitar and Georgie Fame's Hammond. Morrison's singing is inspired, and lyrically he seems to be drawing on the memory of the Christian songwriter Sydney Carter, best known for 'Lord Of The Dance'.

'Avalon Sunset' winds down with the reflective 'These Are The Days', another Van song that seems to balance the spiritual with the carnal, but ultimately comes down on the side of The Big Man. It is an instructive song to study: lyrically there is little new, there is no past and no future, "there's only now" and these are the days we must learn to savour... But in Morrison's hands, his brooding vocal and total involvement in the song, carry the listener along, and as he drifts na-na-na-ing into the sunset, you are left with the memory of a transcendent moment, at the conclusion of a truly satisfactory sequence of songs.

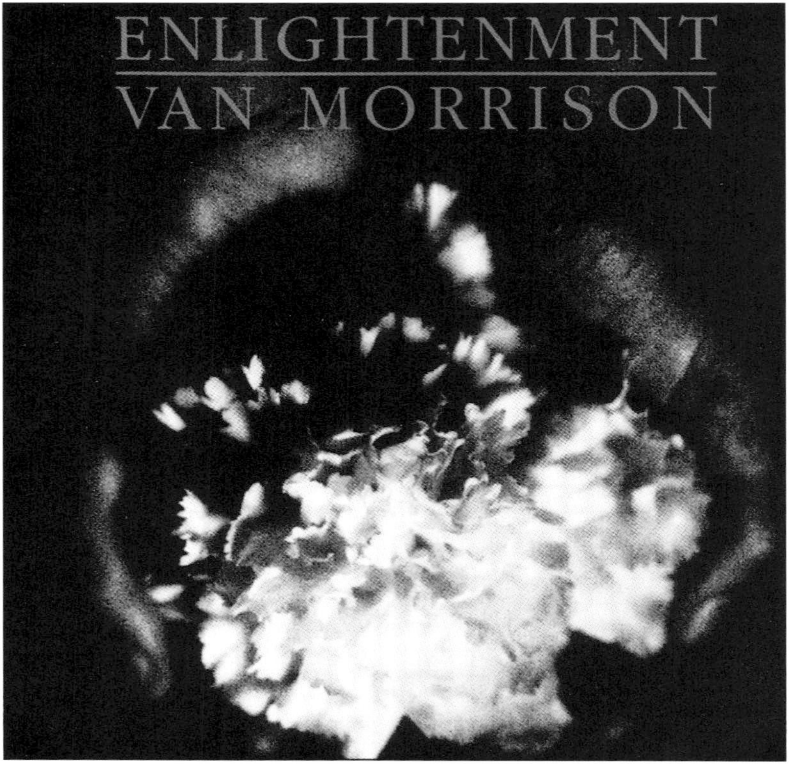
ENLIGHTENMENT
VAN MORRISON

ENLIGHTENMENT

(POLYDOR 847 100–2, SEPTEMBER 1990)

After the heights soared by 'Avalon Sunset', it came as no real surprise that 'Enlightenment' failed to build on its predecessor's triumph. At times, the new album actually sounded uncomfortably close to a tracing of 'Avalon Sunset'.

By the time of 'Enlightenment''s release, Morrison was touring regularly, featuring Georgie Fame as an integral member of his live band. Now in his mid-forties and established as a living rock legend, he did little to enhance his reputation. Live shows weaved erratically between the catastrophic and the triumphant, albums wavered. But hell, the fans reasoned, this was par for the course for Van The Man.

'Enlightenment' is saved from being a complete rout by three songs: 'Real Real Gone', 'In The Days Before Rock'n'Roll' and 'Memories'; otherwise the album is Van By The Yard. The title track has Van searching again and truculently admitting he doesn't know what 'Enlightenment' is. 'Avalon Of The Heart' is a return to Arthurian myth, but as Van sings that he's "goin' down to Avalon" to make a brand new start, there is a feeling that this may be a journey he has made one too many times.

'Start All Over Again' is an undemanding jazz effort, while 'She's My Baby' is old fashioned and incongruous – to hear Van sing "she's my lady, she's my baby" in 1990 is a tad embarrassing. 'Youth Of 1,000 Summers' strives to be profound, but doesn't get beyond the starting block, it's Van repeating for the sake of repetition. The song doesn't build and fails to suggest anything more than a vague idea allowed to outstay its welcome.

The lengthy 'So Quiet In Here' does, however, go some way to recapturing the mood of vintage earlier work. Setting the scene with foghorns blowing in the night and salty sea breezes, Van soon sets off looking for another

paradise – the beating heart of his love, a glass of wine with friends... "this must be what paradise is like".

It's 'Real Real Gone' which kicks the album open, with Van namechecking soul giants Solomon Burke, Wilson Pickett, James Brown and Gene ('Duke Of Earl') Chandler. The song has the same breezy, brassy punch as the R&B flavoured 'Domino' of 20 years before.

'Memories', like the previous album's 'Have I Told You Lately', is another of those ballads which Van can conjure up on request. Except that I think

'Memories' is a superior song to the hit. Buoyed by a church hall-style harmonium, the song is atmospheric; and whereas before Van has too often let lacklustre lyrics float on a forgettable tune, here the tune is as supportive as an ocean. 'Memories' acts as a suitably nostalgic epitaph to the whole record.

'In The Days Before Rock'n'Roll' – an extraordinary track even by the gnomic and inscrutable standards of Van Morrison – is what ultimately stops 'Enlightenment' being "just another Van Morrison album". Even those accustomed to the opaque world and nuances of Van, were stumped by this collaboration with poet Paul Durcan, whose voice also narrates the song. Who for example was "Justin", and why are his whereabouts such a mystery? Why does jockey Lester Piggott feature so prominently? And above all, why is such importance attached to the fact that they "let the goldfish go"?

Durcan is an Irish poet, who had published 10 volumes of verse by the time he came to record with his contemporary. To *Q* in 1991, Durcan confessed that: "rock'n'roll is in my bloodstream, just as I imagine it is in many other people's of my generation". Attributing the collaboration to "improvisation and technique", Durcan himself was equally stumped about the ubiquitous Justin – "I don't know".

Inscrutability aside, 'In The Days Before Rock'n'Roll' is an enchanting and captivating memoir of an adolescence spent – ear pressed to the wireless – hearing the clarion call of rock'n'roll pumped out on Radio Luxembourg. Hilversum, Helvetia, Athlone... the song is a litany of all those magical sounding names, which stood out in gold on the dial, as it swept the ether, desperately trying to snatch the sound of American rock'n'roll from out of the airwaves of Europe.

It's a rich and rewarding journey, an eight minute delight, especially when Van swings in to sing the title refrain. But even now, all these years on, I still wonder: just what is it about those goldfish?

VAN MORRISON

Hymns To The Silence

HYMNS TO THE SILENCE

(POLYDOR 849 026–2, SEPTEMBER 1991)

Van fans were used to surprises, they had after all recently witnessed Morrison duetting with Cliff Richard, but eyebrows were raised even further by the release of a new album by Las Vegas hip-swiveller Tom Jones – featuring four tracks written by Van Morrison! The 1991 release 'Carrying A Torch' was a "comeback" album from the Welsh wizard, intended to build on the credibility he had gained with his 1988 hit version of Prince's 'Kiss', recorded with The Art Of Noise.

'Carrying A Torch' had Jones The Voice working out on songs by The Waterboys, Diane Warren, John Parr... and four specially written for him by Van Morrison. The Morrison songs were laid down in a speedy four hour session, following a phone call from Van to Tom. Later Jones proudly told *Vox* magazine: "Being in the studio with Van Morrison was the best feeling I've had on a recording session since the early days." Those "early days" included spells when Them and Jones shared a label – Decca, as well as some gigs on the Top Rank circuit of the mid–Sixties. The four songs: 'Carrying A Torch', 'Some Peace Of Mind', 'I'm Not Feeling It Anymore' and 'It Must Be You', were also to appear on the latest Van Morrison album, 'Hymns To The Silence'.

This was Morrison's first double album since the live, 'It's Too Late To Stop Now', nearly 20 years before. Fans had long given up second-guessing Van, but still it was a mystery quite why he felt this collection had enough strong songs to merit stretching over two CDs. As is often the case with double albums, a sensible cull of the 21 songs would have resulted in a much stronger, single album. And another thing: what prompted the Theosophic-Scientological-Mystical-Jehovah's Witness, the constantly spiritually-questing Morrison, to include two old-fashioned, no-questions-asked, blind faith, Christian hymns ('Just A

Closer Walk With Thee' and 'Be Thou My Vision') on a rock'n'roll album?

'Hymns To The Silence' kicked off with a familiar Morrison mood: misunderstood. 'Professional Jealousy' was at pains to depict how hard done by Van was – dogged by jealousy, "personal invasion", black propaganda, lies, bitterness and anger; before concluding that the only way to deal with these intrusions is to deliver "the product on time". It was a familiar Morrison complaint, and was by now becoming a mite wearisome.

Things picked up with 'I'm Not Feeling It Anymore', a gentle, floating melody, with Van bopping away on top. Lyrically though he wasn't pulling any fresh rabbits out of the hat – the singer has lost his peace of mind, the idea that fame brings you happiness is an illusion, the only happiness is within... You know the score.

'I'm Not Feeling It Anymore' is one of the better songs on 'Hymns To The Silence', but hearing Morrison sing "the truth will set you free" is only to hear

one side of the story. Morrison seems to dictate the truth, in the same way that the victor always writes the history of a war; but ultimately his perception of the truth is just that – Van Morrison's version of the truth.

The bluesy 'Ordinary Life' tips towards the ordinary, while 'Some Peace Of Mind' slips into the cosy familiarity of Morrison's work with Georgie Fame, whose piping organ fills are beginning to sound tiresome. 'So Complicated' opens with a swinging horn section, and ends with Van bemoaning that all he wants to do is "blow his horn". It was around this time that Morrison began to play with big bands and emphasise his interest in jazz, as opposed to the pop, R&B and folk which had featured so prominently earlier in his career.

Morrison had also begun redefining his blues roots. From around 1991, he made regular appearances at The King's Hotel in Newport, Gwent. This ordinary hotel, just over the Clifton Suspension Bridge in Wales, became a regular haunt for Morrison, particularly when he was rehearsing for tours. Those lucky enough to have witnessed him playing there, recount with slack-jawed awe, the intensity, commitment and length of those shows.

The now familiar dissatisfaction surfaces again on 'Why Must I Always Explain?', wherein Van bemoans the fact that he has to explain everything, and further more, that when he does, people misunderstand him and his motives. 'Hymns To The Silence' as a whole, is one of Morrison's most self–centred and complaining collections to date.

The first real high on 'Hymns To The Silence' comes courtesy of another collaboration with The Chieftains: 'I Can't Stop Loving You' is Van's take, on a Don Gibson country standard, as put through the R&B mill by Ray Charles.

At the core of 'Hymns To The Silence' is a group of songs recalling more innocent times, when Van was growing up in Hyndford Street. Filtered through Morrison's memories, Belfast 5 – sounding like Eden before the fall – is celebrated on 'See Me Through Part II', 'Take Me Back' and 'On Hyndford Street'.

'See Me Through Part II' is basically the popular hymn 'Just A Closer Walk With Thee', with added "vocal intrusions". Van scats, recalling country great Hank Williams and jazz giant Sidney Bechet, who came into the Morrison family home through the magic of wireless. This was a safe, cosy haven, in simpler times, way back before the complexities of fame, back even before the days of rock'n'roll.

'Take Me Back' does just that for the listener. Back to golden summer afternoons of youth, and the cold dark nights of adolescence, with so much soul coming out of the radio. And all the while, the big boats go steaming by... But there is more to this song than just reconstructed memories: the Van of now looks back at the young George Ivan of then, recognising wistfully that "everything felt so right and so good".

'Take Me Back' recognises the

timeless, eternal moment. Moments like those celebrated by Evelyn Waugh near the beginning of 'Brideshead Revisited', and by Morrison himself only a few years before, when he asked rhetorically: "wouldn't it be great if it was like this all the time?"

The second disc opens promisingly with 'By His Grace', featuring strong vocal support from the ubiquitous Carol Kenyon and the smoky Georgie Fame. But by the second song, 'All Saints Day', Fame's familiar Hammond begins to grate, and the throwaway song soon concludes.

The 10 minute title track never quite attains the epic Morrison magic of, say 'Listen To The Lion'. 'Hymns To The Silence' is too subdued, and harks unsatisfactorily back to the accomplished grandeur of 'Common One' and 'Beautiful Vision'.

'Carrying A Torch' feels like one of those effortless, and tellingly accurate, self—contained songs which Van Morrison can conjure up with consummate ease. It lacks the sustained vigour

of 'Into The Mystic' or 'Cry For Home', but at least suggests the possibility of a return to those vintage heights.

The rest of the album dips down and out, sounding like Morrison lost interest in the project. 'Green Mansions' set high upon a hill, lacks the keening sense of wonder which Hank Williams and Bruce Springsteen had brought to the mansions on their respective hills. While 'Pagan Streams' just has Morrison sounding ill—humoured at being unable to locate any white horses. Neither 'It Must Be You', nor 'I Need Your Kind Of Loving', do much to balance out the unevenness of 'Hymns To The Silence' – if anything, they suggest that Van The Man is becoming Van The Bland. And while 'Quality Street' may be impassioned and intense, the listener is still irresistibly reminded of a tin of chocolates.

Overall, 'Hymns To The Silence' was a curate's egg of a collection; it introduced two further regulars to the Van Morrison family – saxophonist Candy Dulfer and multi—instrumentalist Kate St John, but the most striking song from the two discs is the five minute plus, spoken slice of autobiography, 'On Hyndford Street'. Here, what strikes most immediately is that burring growl of a voice, a voice born out of the streets of Belfast, and wearied by experience in America, finally returning back from exile to his home.

Mesmerising as 'On Hyndford Street' undoubtedly is, it begs the question of why Morrison continues to be so openly and directly autobiographical? While one half of the man moans about the intrusiveness of the media, filleting his private life for the delectation of readers, the other half repeatedly lays himself open with the patently autobiographical material he records.

'On Hyndford Street' is a litany of just who the young Van Morrison was, as well as the places that made him. The streets around his home, the images and precious fragments of a childhood long gone, they are all here. 'On Hyndford Street' is the Morrison equivalent of Marcel Proust's madeleine, bitten into, it immediately releases all the sensations of youth. Here is Van remembering the pylon visible at the end of the road; late night Luxembourg and early morning BBC Third Programme; the tree–lined streets of Cyprus Avenue; the railway journey from 'Madame George'; the questing comfort of Jack Kerouac...

'On Hyndford Street' is Van Morrison's Ulysses. Like Joyce's novel, his memories of home and childhood are filtered through fond exile. In Morrison's case, his journey is stalked by The Chieftains' Derek Bell, whose eerie synthesiser is a constant companion. It is an accomplished piece of storytelling, and as poignant an evocation of the end of the innocence as you are ever likely to get.

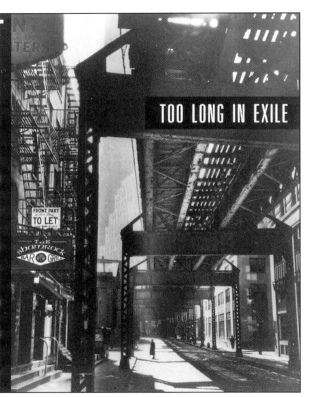

TOO LONG IN EXILE

(POLYDOR 519 219–2, MAY 1993)

For all his evident dislike of the music business, his loathing for the rock'n'roll circus, his mistrust of the media, his rollercoaster live performances and a willingness to dispatch himself into exile, Van Morrison has always given good value to his fans. Aside from the three year absence between 'Veedon Fleece' and 'A Period Of Transition', Van has almost without fail, released an album of new material every year. And to promote the new album, Morrison will tour, allowing fans the opportunity to hear him stretching out on new songs, as well as cherrypicking his back catalogue.

Live performances may veer from the majestic to the mundane, but there is little doubting Morrison's commitment to his music. There is no arbitrary cutting off a period of his career, or point–blank refusal to play certain songs; the arrangements may differ, and latterly Van may elect to have Brian Kennedy sing rather than take the vocal himself, but with Van Morrison, what you see is what you get.

'Too Long In Exile' had Van on a funkier, bluesier jag, and obviously content with his music at the time, the CD was pushed to the limit, with 77 minutes playing time. Where 'Hymns To The Silence' had been contemplative and introspective, 'Too Long In Exile' was confident and outgoing.

Maybe it was the fact that of 15 pieces on the CD, five were cover versions, one was an adaptation of a Yeats poem and another found Van revisiting his biggest hit. Or maybe it was to do with his new collaborator – in the footsteps of Cliff Richard and Tom Jones, came John Lee Hooker. Van had guested on the veteran bluesman's second "comeback" album, 1991's 'Mr Lucky', and Hooker was a formative influence stretching way back to the streets of Belfast. At 75, Hooker still sounded as dynamic and sinister as at any time during his career, which had begun in the blues clubs of Cincinatti and Chicago in the Thirties. Hooker had been making records for nearly half a century when he duetted with Van on Them's 'Gloria' and the heartfelt 'Wasted Years'.

The blues feel of the album was furthered by Morrison's inclusion of Sonny Boy Williamson's 'Good Morning Little Schoolgirl'. The song had been a staple of the Sixties British R&B boom, with cover versions recorded by The Yardbirds, Ten Years After and Rod Stewart, it also featured in the repertoire of the Rolling Stones, Them and The Animals.

Most intriguing of the other covers on 'Too Long In Exile', was the Doc Pomus classic 'Lonely Avenue'. Written for Ray Charles, Los Lobos handled it hauntingly on the touching 1995 Pomus tribute album 'Till The Night Is Gone'. Van's version is suitably brooding, but spoilt by his insistence on doing that bubbling thing with his mouth. This hallmark Morrison vocal mannerism can irritate beyond belief, and while

presumably intended to imply soul, it yet again suggests the sound of a fish submerging for the last time.

Brook Benton's 'I'll Take Care Of You' was an R&B hit for Bobby Bland; 'Moody's Mood For Love' had been written by former Dizzy Gillespie saxophonist James Moody; while the joyous 'The Lonesome Road' had previously seen service in the hands of Fats Waller and Tommy Dorsey. 'Before The World Was Made' – from a text by W.B.Yeats – was set to a smooth jazz backing by Kenny Craddock.

Of the new Morrison compositions, the most arresting was 'Big Time Operators', a slice of autobiography recounting Van's experiences with Bert Berns' Bang Records in New York in 1967. What made the nearly 50 year-old Morrison reflect, in such bitter detail, on events of a quarter of a century before, Van alone knows. Certainly young musicians in the Sixties were systematically ripped off, but did "they" really go to the lengths Morrison ascribes in this song – tapping his phone, trying to get him deported, threatening to have him busted for drugs?

While there were suggestions that there was little new on 'Too Long In Exile', Morrison's revisiting of familiar themes and moods had at least an air of freshness. But the eight minute 'Till We Get The Healing Done' slipped into a reflective groove and the title of the appealing short instrumental 'Close Enough For Jazz' tells you all you need to know about its content.

'Ball & Chain' had one of the album's best melodies and one of its most intriguing lyrics. Van pleaded to be bound, tired of a life which he tellingly calls "a fugitive dream", Van is reborn by the promise of true love.

'Too Long In Exile' itself, is another of those marvellous Van grooves, a platform on which to build. The beguiling melody entices you in, as Van riffs on Thomas Wolfe (you can't go home again), Bob Dylan (like a rolling stone) and the agony of the Irish and their tendency to exile. The Morrison list of those Irish figureheads who have departed Erin's green shore is predictably prestigious: James Joyce, Oscar Wilde, Samuel Beckett — although he momentarily takes his eye off the ball by adding George Best and Alex Higgins.

It was James Joyce who wrote in *A Portrait Of The Artist As A Young Man:* "I will try to express myself in some mode of life or art as freely as I can, using for my defence the only arms I allow myself to use, silence, exile and cunning."

VAN MORRISON   DAYS LIKE THIS

DAYS LIKE THIS

(POLYDOR 527 307–2, JUNE 1995)

The Big One. 'Days Like This' was nominated for the Mercury Music Prize, and Polydor busily promoted the album prior to the presentation on September 12, 1995. Van was a 10/1 outsider, and in the end – along with Oasis, P.J. Harvey, Elastica, Leftfield, Tricky, James Macmillan, Supergrass and Guy Barker – he lost out to Portishead.

However, the success of the 'Best Of Van Morrison' compilation had made a wider audience aware of his work, and that interest carried on over to 'Days Like This' which entered the chart at No 5, only four places below Michael Jackson's 'History'. Suddenly, following the Lifetime Achievement Award he received at the 1994 Brits, and with his name being dropped by all the right people, in all the right places, Van Morrison was back in fashion with a vengeance.

Personally, Van seemed to have found a degree of contentment in his highly visible relationship with Michelle Rocca, a former Miss Ireland with whom Van was wont to walk out. Seasoned Van-watchers attributed The Man's new-found bonhomie to Ms Rocca's influence, and she even steered him towards some high fashion shops to get him togged up for the Nineties. Van was soon cutting a dapper little figure around town, a dashing fedora never far from his head.

Publicly too, Van was in demand. In December 1995, Belfast poet Gerald Dawe hosted a conversation with Morrison about his songwriting technique at a Literature Festival in Swansea. Dawe came from the same streets as Van, and in a piece for *The Irish Times,* the poet recalled: "We went to Sammy Houston's Jazz Club, Betty Staffs, the Maritime, the Rikki Tikki Club, the Floral Hall, the Orpheus, the Fiesta, King George Hall. A large chunk of our lives was devoted to listening to music, dancing to it and buying it. Music was our life and Belfast was full of it:

R&B, folk, rock, jazz and pop." Such affinity went sadly unrealised onstage, Van muttered and mumbled, and – in the words of another enigmatic poet – "nothing was revealed".

Musically, Van was still making the most of his relationship with Georgie Fame, and there were plenty of rumours about a jazz album the two were planning. On record, Kate St John, Candy Dulfer and Pee Wee Ellis were among the familiar names on Van album sleeves, while in concert, backing vocalist Brian Kennedy was now, quite literally, sharing the spotlight with Morrison. The presence of Brian Kennedy on 'Days Like This' was anticipated, but his ubiquity was not welcomed. Live, Kennedy helped take some of the pressure off Van's vocals, but his presence on disc was superfluous. He seemed to haunt Van like a ghost at the feast, every Morrison utterance shadowed by Kennedy, Van is never left alone. 'Melancholia', 'No Religion' and 'Ancient Highway' particularly are dogged by Kennedy's carbon–paper vocals.

Van himself was well pleased with the finished album. In a series of interviews – conducted for convenience sake, by Michelle Rocca – he confessed that he found 'Days Like This' his most satisfying studio album since 'Enlightenment', although titles such as 'Underlying Depression', 'Melancholia' and 'Russian Roulette' suggested his frame of mind was otherwise when he was writing for the record.

There was a lot to admire on 'Days Like This', but the acclaim which greeted it was out of proportion to the quality of the music it contained. The two covers were pleasant, for a number of reasons. 'You Don't Know Me' was a song Van used to sing with The Monarchs in the dim and distant pre-Them days in Belfast. Written by country singer Eddy Arnold, the song was made popular by Ray Charles, whose version of 'I Can't Stop Loving You' Morrison also performed with The Monarchs around that time. Van's version of 'You Don't Know Me' on 'Days Like This', was a duet with his daughter Shana, who was beginning her own career as a singer-songwriter, the evidence on her father's record suggested a promising career.

Morrison first remembered hearing 'I'll Never Be Free' – the second duet with Shana on the album – on a record by Tennessee Ernie Ford & Kay Starr, which his father owned. Van is believed to have recorded other covers at the sessions, some of which remain unreleased, including 'I Don't Want To Go On Without You' which had been a hit for The Drifters, and was, intriguingly, co-written by Bert Berns – long the subject of Morrison's wrath, both in print and on record. Also cut was the standard 'That Old Black Magic', which has seen service by everyone from Louis Prima to Frank Sinatra. Morrison's version was eventually released as a 1995 single; Van takes it at a spritely pace and again duets with his daughter.

Of the remaining 10 Morrison originals, 'Raincheck' was the now predictable rant against the crooks who populate the music industry. Morrison had vented his spleen more specifically on 'Big Time Operators' for his previous album, and to hear him spend a further six minutes in similar vein here, insisting that he wouldn't let the bastards grind him down, was unrewarding. 'Songwriter' was a Van-as-working–man song: "don't call me a sage" he pleaded. While the lyrics did admit to a certain technical ability at fashioning words on a page, the composer refused to tote the burden which his songs had become. "Na, na, na...". To Ms Rocca, Van explained that "the thing about songwriting is there are no rules... I mean, you could read a Heinz beans label if you wanted to and change that into poetry. Advertising is just low-grade poetry, that's all."

'Underlying Depression' did little to persuade anyone that Morrison was anything other than a miserable old git, despite the soporific declamation that all Van had was underlying depression. 'Days Like This' limped along, with Van anticipating that there would, indeed, be days like this and, uh, that's about it. Others though, found the song a resilient song of defiance. Following the IRA Ceasefire in 1994, 'Days Like This' was used as the theme of peace by the Northern Ireland Office in a million pound campaign to restore people's confidence in the Province.

'Melancholia' had been touted as a major new Van song by those who had heard him perform it regularly on the dates leading up to the release of 'Days Like This'. But on record, the song suffered from Van's misguided repetition of the title, presumably in the hope of engendering more mood or soul (see also 'Underlying Depression'), and matters were not helped by the foot step-dogging backing vocals.

'No Religion' has Van imagining a world without religion, where the meek don't stand a chance of inheriting anything. The song's sentiments are of interest and it benefits from one of the album's most striking melodies.

Things picked up, but only just in time. The near nine minute 'Ancient Highway', the album's penultimate track, had Van growling his way through

an enticing revisit to the haunts of ancient pieces. The song contained elements of 'Madame George', with its reference to a "trancelike vision", while the evocations of Belfast recalled 'Astral Weeks'. Van even quoted one of his own song titles, 'A Town Called Paradise', back to himself. The folk poet of despair, Hank Williams, made his first appearance in a Morrison song since 'Saint Dominic's Preview' over 20 years before. 'Ancient Highway' was a return to the sort of turf which Van had made his own, a growling, searching odyssey, balancing the sensual and the spiritual, lightly sprinkled with recollections of childhood.

The closing 'In The Afternoon' adds nothing of any real substance, and concludes an album which adds little lustre to the Van Morrison legend. By this stage of his career, after nearly 40 years as a professional musician, Morrison was not alone in finding it difficult to keep inspired and inspiring, recent albums from hardy perennials like Lou Reed and Bob Dylan having demonstrated that their wells were also running dry.

Maybe it was because Van had achieved so much that so much more was expected of him. But he can no more be expected to create an 'Astral Weeks' or 'Saint Dominic's Preview' with each album, than Shakespeare could have been expected to come up with *Hamlet* every time he put quill to parchment. Other distractions were making claims on Morrison's time, and besides, by the time of 'Days Like This', his 22nd solo album, Van really didn't have anything left to prove.

In person, Van Morrison can be at best enigmatic and inscrutable, at worst sullen and surly. The dichotomy is that a man who has produced some of the most exhilarating, consoling and uplifting songs within the framework of popular music can in person be so boorish and insensitive. Journalists who have spent much of their professional lives ably documenting Van's career, have actually been reduced to tears when encountering the man himself in an interview situation.

In a *Q* review to celebrate the 1988 release of his remaining back catalogue on CD, Paul Du Noyer asked the question which has puzzled so many Van fans for 30 or so years: "So why should it be that Morrison, a stubby and stubbornly uncommunicative man, sometimes described as charmless and grumpy by those who've had to deal with him, has amassed a body of work whose grace and emotional potency surpasses almost anything else emerging from within the general vicinity of rock'n'roll?"

Even the keenly anticipated live shows with Ray Charles during mid-1996 failed to spark the old electricity. Van's set was a competent, if perfunctory, 90-minute distillation of his Nineties act. Ray Charles gave only glimpses of his intuitive genius, and fans were bitterly disappointed that the duets were limited to an occasional hasty run through of 'I Believe In My Soul'. For all the talk of soul, there was precious little evidence of it percolating

from the stage.

When the announcement of Van Morrison's nomination for an OBE "for services to music" in John Major's Honours List of June 1996 made front–page news, the rest of the world was alerted to what many already knew. Morrison was apparently one of a number of "people's choices" for the honour. What made it unique was that Van was being honoured solely for his contribution to music – previous pop nominees had received their accolades for charity work.

Van's split with Michelle Rocca at around the same time also put The Man on the front page of the newspapers. From being an intensely private man, whose talent was acknowledged by a fervent group of fans, Van had suddenly become fresh meat for the tabloids. Media frenzy reached its fatuous peak in the *Evening Standard* on June 7, 1996: under the heading "Transit Van", Dee McQuillan traced the footsteps of "pop legend" Van Morrison around Notting Hill ("he's been spotted in the park walking, and shopping at the Europa supermarket").

It was all a mighty long way from the terraced house on Hyndford Street. Across the stage of Belfast's Maritime Hotel to the world with Them; from Cyprus Avenue to Woodstock; from Coney Island to Marin County. From a time before rock'n'roll to a world embracing folk, jazz, R&B and blues. And all courtesy of one man – George Ivan Morrison, OBE. Fifty plus, and still raging hard, it truly is too late to stop now.

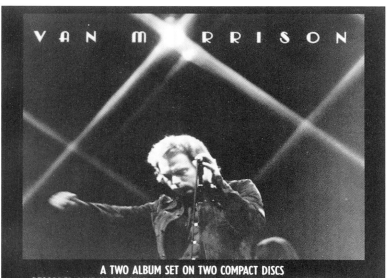

A TWO ALBUM SET ON TWO COMPACT DISCS
RECORDED LIVE IN CONCERT • LOS ANGELES AND LONDON • SUMMER 1973

LIVE ALBUMS

IT'S TOO LATE TO STOP NOW

(POLYDOR 839 166-2, FEBRUARY 1974)

As a live performer, Van Morrison has often been erratic, veering between the sublime and the ridiculous; but he has always testified that music is his job, and part and parcel of that job is live performance. It's to his credit that Van has always gone out and worked an album, not for him any temperamental hibernation. Also on the plus side, Van has contented himself with playing venues where the audience can actually see the act, the temptation to play aircraft hangars has been consistently resisted and he has never succumbed to the easy option of tour sponsorship ("Guinness Presents Van 'The Man' Morrison In Concert!"). Van likes to settle in at a concert-hall sized venue – Belfast's Grand Opera House or London's Dominion Theatre – for a stint.

At his best, Morrison is a consummate live rock performer: he plays the songs the fans have come to hear; he is willing to take risks on re-arranging and re-interpreting familiar material, to keep it fresh for him and to stimulate interest in long-time fans. He will improvise, which – on a good night – can result in some of the most exhilarating brinksmanship in rock'n'roll. He will hand-pick a band, which can match his own R&B, folk, jazz, blues and rock heritage and fully interpret his music at its best. He will include a choice selection of cover versions, which indicate just where his own musical tastes were formed. On a good night, Van has even been known to talk and joke with the audience.

In concert, on one of those good nights, Van Morrison is a true artist. Too often, rock legends rely on the cosy familiarity of the past, churning out a

Greatest Hits package, with little or no deviation from the all too familiar recorded versions. Or they will use the concert stage as a platform for fresh and unfamiliar material, only grudgingly recognising that the audience are there, and reluctantly tossing them a few crumbs of comfort in the shape of old favourites.

Van veers between the two extremes. He has been responsible for some of the most uplifting nights of music I have ever heard in a concert hall, but he is equally capable of dismissing his audience with a performance so ill-tempered and off-hand, that you determine never to go out of your way to see him perform ever again... But five years later, you realise you haven't seen the old feller in concert for a while, and all you remember are the good times, so you start again on that same old roller coaster ride.

Morrison's truculence accompanies him everywhere on the road, a 1987 account had his personal chef making him a special sandwich every night, which every night Morrison refused to touch. "Playing live is not touring," Morrison told Chris Salewicz. "Touring is carrying a lot of bags around and taking a lot of flights and waiting in airports. That's what touring is. It's nothing to do with playing."

As far as Van live on disc is concerned, his first live set, 'It's Too Late To Stop Now', is unquestionably one of the best-ever live rock'n'roll recordings. The title comes from the line Morrison sings at the fade of the original 'Into The Mystic' from 'Moondance'. Van was cooking when he came to record these 18 songs, coming between 'Hard Nose The Highway' and 'Veedon Fleece', 'It's Too Late To Stop Now' had Van fronting The Caledonia Soul Orchestra, arguably his finest ever ensemble. Caledonia – aka Scotland – was the only part of Britain not conquered by the Romans, and the name occupies a special place in the Morrison story, Morrison called his Eighties production company Caledonia, and George &

Violet Morrison's record store was also called Caledonia. Incorporating long-time cohorts Dahaud Shaar on drums and John Platania on guitar, as well as bassist David Hayes and keyboard man Jeff Labes, the orchestra also boasted a five person string section and a two man horn duo – imagine the cost of mounting a touring band like that today.

On its original release, 'It's Too Late To Stop Now' was soon cemented as one of the great rock'n'roll double albums – light years ahead of Crosby, Stills, Nash & Young's 'Four Way Street'; streets ahead of Bob Dylan's 'Before The Flood' and 'At Budokan'. Only The Band's 'Rock Of Ages' and Joni Mitchell's 'Miles Of Aisles' could contend.

By the time he came to release 'It's Too Late To Stop Now', Morrison had been touring professionally for over a decade, he had – in the phraseology of the time – paid his dues. Confident of his own abilities, certain of the quality of his ensemble, Morrison had the confidence to make this record. A measure of that confidence is that every note you hear was recorded live – there was not one overdub, though sadly this meant that 'Moondance' had to be dropped because of one bum note.

Looking back on the album, guitarist John Platania told *Mojo:* "I would say that tour represented the height of his confidence as a performer", while bassist David Hayes recalled: "When I speak to Van about that album he still talks about it as having marked the peak of his career. He really feels he was on to something very special."

Of course, a live album is meant to be just that – a souvenir of a concert performance – but rock'n'roll's quest for "authenticity" has seen certain well-known rock bands record their "live" albums at studios on the outskirts of London without an audience in sight, the enthusiastic response to be added on afterwards, like the manipulative TV director in *Annie Hall,* carefully dubbing a laughter track onto his comedy efforts: "Can we start with a slow chuckle there, then build to a guffaw?"

With 'It's Too Late To Stop Now', what you hear is what you get. The album acts as a Van Morrison Greatest Hits ('Domino', 'Here Comes The Night', 'Gloria'); it stands as a career overview, 1965-1973; and it even includes a selection of songs from the young Van's jukebox, with covers of songs by Bobby Bland, Ray Charles, Sam Cooke, Willie Dixon and Sonny Boy Williamson.

Recorded in Los Angeles at the intimate Troubadour club and the Santa Monica Civic Theatre, as well as at North London's Rainbow, 'It's Too Late To Stop Now' kicks off with a take on Bobby Bland's 'Ain't Nothin' You Can Do', before dipping into a cosy 'Warm Love' and muscular 'Into The Mystic'. The concluding track on Disc 1, Willie Dixon's 'I Just Want To Make Love To You' was Van revisiting his teenage R&B roots. The song, a staple of every spotty, fledgling Brit-band's repertoire, was recorded by Johnny Kidd & The Pirates, The Animals and The Rolling Stones, and before them by Chuck

Berry, Bo Diddley, Muddy Waters and Etta James.

The sound of Disc 1 of 'It's Too Late To Stop Now' was bluesy and brassy, economical versions of the bluesy side of Van. Disc 2 brought the string section to prominence, and emphasised the more pioneering spirit of Morrison, with inspired readings of 'Saint Dominic's Preview', 'Listen To The Lion' and 'Cyprus Avenue'.

'Listen To The Lion', in particular, has Morrison lost in a reverie of sorts. His vocal mannerisms, which can on occasion be irritating, are here married to the music, and you can hear him becoming slowly engrossed by and wrapped up in his self-created music right down to what is probably the greatest live 'fade-out' ever recorded.

'Here Comes The Night' receives an ecstatic reception, not only because it was Morrison's biggest UK hit, but because the use of the strings on stage was all the more dramatic at the time. The use of Moog synthesisers to replicate the sound of an orchestra was by then commonplace, and to witness the compact string section of The Caledonia Soul Orchestra sawing away was a sight for sore eyes in the early Seventies.

'Caravan' steamrollers into soul, while 'Cyprus Avenue' is transformed from a meditative, contemplative stroll, into a bluesy swagger, before dipping back into a jaunt backed by strings. Its 10 minute sweep is a complete distillation of just what made Van Morrison so magnificent a performer way back then. "Turn it on, Van!" someone calls out from the audience near the song's end. "It's turned on already," announces Morrison smugly. And he was right.

VAN MORRISON

Live At The Grand Opera House Belfast

LIVE AT THE GRAND OPERA HOUSE BELFAST

(POLYDOR 839 602–2, FEBRUARY 1984)

Ten years down the line, 'Live At The Grand Opera House Belfast' acted as a statement of where Morrison was at with his music now. The 11 tracks concentrated on the albums of the past five years, and aside from a brief instrumental snatch of 'Into The Mystic', there was nothing prior to 1979's 'Into The Music' album.

In truth, the versions of recent songs on 'Live At The Grand Opera House Belfast' differed little from their studio counterparts: a soulful Van fronting a familiar ensemble – saxophone, trumpet, keyboards, bass, drums, guitar and a trio of backing vocalists.

The exceptions were 'Full Force Gale', which came across as punchier than its album original, and an extended version of 'Rave On John Donne', which gains in striking performance what it loses in mystical power.

Perhaps more was expected from Morrison's first live album recorded in his home city of Belfast, but at least some of that excitement and anticipation is conveyed on the concluding, autobiographical, 'Cleaning Windows'.

VAN MORRISON

a night in san francisco

recorded live at the Masonic Auditorium San Francisco

PORT OF

SAN FRANCISCO

A NIGHT IN SAN FRANCISCO

(POLYDOR 521290–2, APRIL 1994)

Another decade, another live Van Morrison album. This double CD, 22 track package, celebrated Morrison's style of performance in the Nineties. Over two and a half hours of music replicated, as near as dammit, a Van Morrison show. "Ballads, blues, soul, funk & jazz" boasted the back sleeve, but "jazz" is what emerged head and shoulders above the pack.

The line-up recorded at San Francisco's Masonic Auditorium late in 1993, was horn heavy (Haji Ahkba, Kate St John, Candy Dulfer), and erred heavily on the jazz side of things. 'A Night In San Francisco' is a good enough souvenir of a slice of Van's performing life, but it wears thin after repeated playing.

Morrison MCs, and almost as if to stress the jazz "authenticity", introduces each soloist to the audience after their party piece. This is a jazz hallmark, which in concert may have been informative but on disc is simply frustrating.

There is a perfunctory trawl through the Morrison catalogue, enlivened by a snappy 'I've Been Working', and Georgie Fame solos beautifully on 'I Forgot That Love Existed' – which ends with an uncredited rockin' fade on Dylan's 'All Along The Watchtower'.

Too often though, Morrison's vocals are mumbled and muddled, inaudibility masquerading as soul. Then there are the guests... Brian Kennedy has a pleasant voice, on his own material. But here his frequent duets with Morrison only detract from his master's voice, and on 'You Make Me Feel So Free', makes Van into a guest on his own song. The feeling that listeners want the engineer, and not the oily rag, is never stronger than on 'Tupelo Honey', a rare enough song for Van to revisit, but what we get is Kennedy's anodyne cover. Ultimately it is Morrison who is at fault for letting the supporting cast take the spotlight. It is Van who has the final say, and his

PAGE 123

voice is all but muffled here.

'Moondance' is pitched a mite fast but at least Van sounds in control, Teena Lyle's vibes are appropriately groovy, and the segue into 'My Funny Valentine' works better than any other transition on the set.

Too often 'A Night In San Francisco' goes on automatic: the band grooves along, powered by dual keyboards, punctuated by saxophone, which has a soporific effect. The quotes from familiar songs don't sound as if they have grown organically, but rather as if they've been gratuitously grafted onto Morrison's originals. Van borrows heavily – 'Ain't That Loving You Baby?' from Jimmy Reed; Sly Stone's 'Thank You...'; Sonny Boy Williamson's 'Help Me' and 'Good Morning Little Schoolgirl'; T–Bone Walker's 'Stormy Monday'; Booker T's 'Green Onions'; James Brown's 'It's A Man's Man's Man's World'; Sam Cooke's 'You Send Me'; everybody's 'My Funny Valentine'...

Then dim the lights, and a single spot on the guests. And what guests they were:

John Lee Hooker, out to replicate his duet on 'Gloria', Junior Wells and Jimmy Witherspoon. The veteran bluesmen are wheeled out, but there is still little sense of a real event; at no time do you sense any excitement from Morrison at sharing the stage with such legends.

The second CD generally fares better, with Van stretching out, particularly on 'Lonely Avenue', in which he remembers Marty Wilde as another radio favourite and takes in a little bit of Gene Vincent and a Jimmy Witherspoon cameo.

Given the all-star cast and brass-heavy bias, it is the more subdued songs at the end of the disc which work best: 'So Quiet In Here', and the extended 'In The Garden' which inspires Morrison to his best vocal performance on the set. Things pick up speed come encore time, with a feisty take on Johnny Kidd & The Pirates 'Shakin' All Over', which slips cosily into a spirited 'Gloria' boasting cameos from John Lee Hooker and the beautifully enunciating Kate St John.

Again, as with the previous decade's 'Live In Belfast', the weakness of 'A Night

In San Francisco' was that it presented the bluesier, brassier side of Van Morrison live, which can be uplifting and exhilarating in performance, but dips after repeated play on disc. The strength of 'It's Too Late To Stop Now' was that it emphasised Morrison's undoubted pop strengths as well as his R&B and folk roots. But all that was dead and buried by the time Van arrived for 'A Night In San Francisco'.

how
long
has this
been
going on

VAN MORRISON

with georgie
fame
& friends

HOW LONG HAS THIS BEEN GOING ON

(VERVE 529 136–2, DECEMBER 1995)

Van Morrison had long talked about cutting a jazz album, but things got seriously underway during the summer of 1995 and proceeded apace on The Autumn Jazz Tour. For the first time, Van's touring band had no featured guitarist, so all the reliance was on keyboards and pronounced horns.

In jazz parlance, Van's band had the chops. 'How Long Has This Been Going On' is the album Van wanted to make, cut "live" at Ronnie Scott's – though without an audience – you can almost picture the smoky, dark interior of Ronnie's Soho jazz sanctuary when you listen to the album.

Even the most familiar Van Morrison titles here are used as an opportunity for extended soloing in the jazz tradition: the seven minute 'Moondance' is basically a platform for extended sax and trumpet workouts. It is a testament to the sureness of Morrison's touch that his original compositions – particularly 'I Will Be There' and 'All Saint's Day' – fit comfortably alongside the jazz standards he selected to cover. Although 'Heathrow Shuffle' which had been writ-

ten during Van's 1974-77 absence, was fairly undistinguished.

Talking to jazz journalist John Fordham while promoting the album, Van admitted that the whole thing was cut in five hours one afternoon, and that Anthony Newley's show-tune standard 'Who Can I Turn To?' was his favourite vocal performance on the record.

"I heard jazz because my father had a huge record collection," Van told Fordham, "and so I heard all this music playing constantly in the background... I thought everybody must have heard this stuff, to me it was like breathing... I came out of the jazz and blues scene in Belfast... I just got caught up in the whole commercial thing, because that's what was happening in the Sixties..."

'How Long Has This Been Going

On' was soused in jazz, and as the realisation of a heartfelt project, it obviously works for Van. He covers songs made popular by Louis Jordan, Lester Young and Mose Allison, while jazz chanteuse Annie Ross makes a subdued guest appearance on 'Blues Backstage'.

The success of 'How Long Has This Been Going On' basically depends on how fond you are of jazz. At its best, the album conveys a popular image of jazz, with earnest young men in berets "digging the groove", as cool chicks in tight dresses stand by drinking espresso coffee. And everyone's smoking like mad. A snapshot of a time, in the days before rock'n'roll.

On into his sixth decade, in concert Van continues to rock and roll his gypsy soul. *Wavelength* magazine reported open-mouthed the accounts of Morrison's four New York Supper Club shows of April 1996. By all accounts a tired and emotional Van delivered some of the most spellbinding shows of his career, in excess of three hours on two nights, including a 50 minute 'It's A Man's Man's Man's Man's World'.

Whether it was the rumoured break–up with Michelle Rocca, or his own delight with his jazz album, or – who the hell knows – Van was on blistering form. All the old favourites were there, as well as backward glances ('A Town Called Paradise', 'Slim Slow Slider', 'Tupelo Honey') and a powerful new song 'The Healing Game'. Uncharacteristically, Van bantered with the audience, at one point even leaning on the monitors to shake hands with someone in the front row.

COMPILATIONS

For Van Morrison Them "lived and died" on the stage of Belfast's Maritime Hotel. It was here that the fiery singer led the group through a spellbinding series of blues and R&B jams. The incendiary career of Them effectively lasted only a year, with a further 12 months tacked on when Morrison found out he was contractually obligated to Decca Records. It was an intense time for the still-teenage Van; and it was because of Morrison's involvement that – along with their Decca labelmates The Small Faces – Them went on to become one of the most recycled of all the Sixties groups.

Talking through his official mouth-piece Michelle Rocca in 1995, Morrison expressed dissatisfaction with his early recordings: "The first couple of Them albums, there was stuff I wouldn't have done, but we had to do because some-body was paying the cheque. One of them was 'Here Comes The Night'... It's a good song, but I didn't like the way it was deliberately tarted up. 'Brown-Eyed Girl', the same thing... 'Gloria' was differ-ent. 'Gloria' was raw blues. That's okay."

THEM:
THE COLLECTION
(CASTLE CCSCD 131, 1986)

This is the best of the many Them compilations currently available on CD. As well as the hit singles 'Baby Please Don't Go', 'Here Comes The Night' and 'Gloria', the remaining 21 tracks display how a fiery Belfast R&B band metamorphosed into a vehicle for the sombre and thought-provoking songs of their lead singer.

'Gloria' is, of course, the best known punk song of all time. It first appeared on the B-side of Them's second single, 'Baby Please Don't Go' in November 1964 and still brings a Van Morrison audience to its feet over 30 years on. The song has been covered by almost everyone, including Jimi Hendrix, The Doors and Patti Smith. Gloria, incidentally, was the name of a young cousin of Morrison's who died when she was 13.

The initial impact of Them came with their pounding cover versions of American R&B favourites – Bobby Bland's 'Turn On Your Love Light' was a storming 15 minute favourite of their Maritime residency, while Ray Charles' 'I Got A Woman', Jimmy Reed's 'Bright

Lights, Big City' and Bobby Troup's 'Route 66' were all in there too. Morrison was already proving himself adept at cover versions – among the highlights of the group's catalogue was a brooding cover of Dylan's 'It's All Over Now Baby Blue', while Paul Simon's 'Richard Cory' proved to be Them's final single.

Among the early champions of Them was DJ Jimmy Savile. To increase Them's chances of commercial success, Decca drafted in American producer Bert Berns, already a legendary name. Berns soon fingered Morrison as the talent in Them, and although it had already been recorded by Lulu, he offered Them his own 'Here Comes The Night'. This

song, complete with unforgettable guitar phrase, cemented the group's short-lived success, and as the group grew in popularity, so Morrison developed as a writer – 'Mystic Eyes', 'Friday's Child' and 'Hey Girl' can be seen as signposts on the road to 'Astral Weeks'.

The problem with Them was that the group still saw themselves as champions of the emerging R&B movement, whereas after the success of 'Here Comes The Night', Decca saw them as a pop group in the tradition of the label's Brian Poole & The Tremeloes or The Zombies.

Bolstered by session players (including the ubiquitous Jimmy Page), Them ended with a whimper rather than an explosion. In the last days of Them, Van got to know his namesake Jim Morrison quite well, and on one memorable occasion joined Jim's new group The Doors on stage at LA's Whiskey A-Go-Go for a 20 minute version of Wilson Pickett's 'In The Midnight Hour'. Back in Belfast during 1966 following the split of Them, Van's outlook was

dim. Various post-Morrison versions of the group continued to tour and record, but the temperamental former singer with a moderately successful R&B band had little to look forward to. Until some bedroom demos cut in Belfast found their way to New York, and out of the blue, a one-way ticket to New York arrived from Bert Berns...

Bert Berns was the stuff of rock'n'roll myth: legend has it that Berns was a nightclub owner in Cuba until he was forced out by Castro following the 1959 revolution. Just like *The Godfather, Part II*. It was Berns who followed Leiber & Stoller as resident writer/producer at Atlantic. And it was Berns who founded Bang Records, which boasted Van Morrison, Neil Diamond and The McCoys.

As a songwriter Bert Berns can also lay claim to at least part-shares of: 'A Little Bit Of Soap' (The Jarmels, Johnny Kidd & The Pirates, Garnet Mimms & The Enchanters, Showaddywaddy); 'Twist & Shout' (The Top Notes, The Beatles, The Isley Brothers, The Who,

Tina Turner, Salt'n'Pepa); 'Cry Baby' (Garnet Mimms & The Enchanters, Janis Joplin, Natalie Cole); 'Tell Him' (The Exciters, Billie Davis, Hello, Linda Ronstadt); 'Everybody Needs Somebody To Love' (Solomon Burke, Rolling Stones, Blues Brothers); 'Hang On Sloopy' (The McCoys, Jimi Hendrix); 'Here Comes The Night' (Them, Lulu, Van Morrison, David Bowie); 'I Want Candy' (The Strangeloves, Brian Poole & The Tremeloes, Bow Wow Wow) and 'Piece Of My Heart' (Big Brother & The Holding Company, Janis Joplin, Bryan Ferry, Etta James, Sammy Hagar).

The only picture I've ever seen of Bert Berns was taken the year he died, and had him looking eerily like Gene Vincent. It was Berns' rheumatic heart which finally did for him in December 1967. "Bert had a tough guy exterior," Neil Diamond recalled, "but he was really a softie."

Van Morrison offers a different opinion. Indeed, he has spent much of his time slagging off Bert Berns in interview, and latterly in song. Whatever the personal conflicts, it was undeniably Berns who recognised that "something" in the singer of Them. It was Berns who got Morrison out of Belfast and it was Berns who oversaw the sessions which produced 'Brown Eyed Girl', which gave Morrison the clout to negotiate with Warner Bros, which led to 'Astral Weeks' and a degree of freedom.

Full track listing: 'Baby Please Don't Go', 'Bright Lights Big City', 'I Put A Spell On You', 'Hello Josophene', 'Turn On Your Love Light', 'Don't Start Crying Now', 'Gloria', 'The Story Of Them', 'It's All Over Now Baby Blue', 'I Gotta Woman', 'My Little Baby', 'How Long Baby', 'Here Comes The Night', 'Stormy Monday', 'I Like It Like That', 'Go On Home Baby', 'Out Of Sight', 'Baby What Do You Want Me To Do', 'Route 66 (Get Your Kicks On)', 'Friday's Child', 'Little Girl', 'Hey Girl', 'Call My Name', 'Mystic Eyes'.

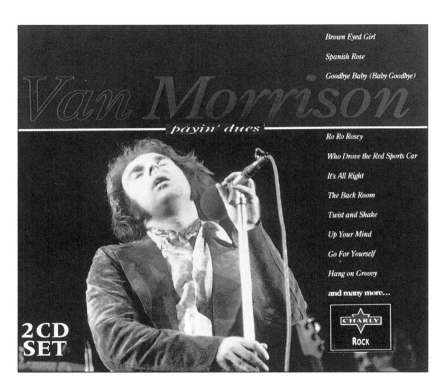

Van Morrison
payin' dues

Brown Eyed Girl

Spanish Rose

Goodbye Baby (Baby Goodbye)

Ro Ro Rosey

Who Drove the Red Sports Car

It's All Right

The Back Room

Twist and Shake

Up Your Mind

Go For Yourself

Hang on Groovy

and many more...

CHARLY
ROCK

2CD SET

PAYIN' DUES
(CHARLY CP CD 8035–2, 1994)

Like Morrison's work with Them, the material he recorded with Bert Berns has been endlessly recycled, but this double CD is the most comprehensive collection. Aside from the more predictable material, it includes one of Morrison's Belfast bedroom demos and an alternate take of 'Brown Eyed Girl'.

Following his success with The McCoys' 'Hang On Sloopy', Berns and his Bang label were looking for hit singles, and agreed to stump up enough for Morrison to record eight songs: four A- and four B-sides. Among the songs recorded at those first New York Bang sessions was what, due to endless recycling on innumerable compilation albums and film soundtracks over the past 30 years, is probably still Van Morrison's best-known song.

'Brown Eyed Girl' began life as a "calypso thing" after Morrison had been reading Lewis Carroll's *Sylvie & Bruno*. An American hit during 1967, the song had to be re-cut when radio censors objected to the line "making love in the green grass", which had to be changed to "laughing and a-running..." (the original "making love"

take can be found on 'Payin' Dues').

The songs on 'Payin' Dues' on which you can detect the hand of Bert Berns are all those around the commercial, three-minute mark: 'Spanish Rose', 'Ro Ro Rosey', 'The Smile You Smile'. Where Morrison's heart really lay is evident on two longer songs he tried out at those 1967 sessions: 'Beside You' and 'Madame George', both of which would reappear – radically reworked – on the following year's 'Astral Weeks'.

With his eye and ear so well-attuned to the commercial marketplace, you can imagine the wariness with which Bert Berns would have listened to the raw, and distinctly uncommercial songs Morrison tried out at his second Bang sessions: 'TB Sheets' and 'Who Drove The Red Sports Car'.

Morrison's experiences with Bert Berns in New York were creatively unrewarding for the young Irishman, despite garnering him an American Top 10 hit in 1967 with 'Brown Eyed Girl'. Van felt that he was battling against unsympathetic studio musicians and an absentee producer.

Of particular interest from those Bang sessions is one of the songs which later found its way onto 'Astral Weeks'. 'Madame George' – arguably one of the finest-ever constructions of pop music in its latter incarnation – is here a beery, brassy "party atmosphere" romp. Other highlights of those sessions include Van's take on the traditional 'Midnight Special', with classy backing vocals from The Sweet Inspirations; the chilling 'TB Sheets'; and the intriguing, Dylan-esque 'Joe Harper Saturday Morning'.

With Warner Bros already expressing interest in Morrison following the success of 'Brown Eyed Girl', and with the artist's dissatisfaction at the way he felt Bert Berns had wilfully mis–promoted him, Morrison was only too keen to quit Bang Records, following Berns' untimely death

at the end of 1967. But Morrison was obliged to deliver a statutory number of sides to Bang before they would let him out of his contract, and these are the 31 "songs" (few of which run to over 60 seconds) which make up the second disc of 'Payin' Dues'.

The sleeve notes breathlessly speak of Van taking Berns' 'Twist & Shout' and trying out "a number of adaptations: 'Twist & Shake', 'Shake & Roll', 'Stomp & Scream', 'Scream & Holler', 'Jump & Thump'... all variations on the same theme, accompanying himself on acoustic guitar, Van Morrison turns Berns' song upside down, inside out and every which-a-way".

Later, Van tries out fragments like 'Goodbye George', 'Dum Dum George', 'Here Comes Dumb George'. "Could all these Georges have synthesised into 'Madame George'?" ask the album compilers. Well, no actually. These Morrison fragments are simply him applying the letter of the law, to ease himself out of what he regarded as an unendurable contract. In one of the most ruthless moves of his career, Morrison discharged his duties to Bang by delivering a series of "songs" which he knew could never be released, but which fulfilled his contractual obligations.

Bert Berns' widow Eileen revealed the true facts to Steve Turner: "He turned over a tape to me that he must have spent a few minutes making... You could never have copyrighted them... he sang something about 'I gotta go in and cut this stupid song for this stupid lady'... I had two small babies, one of them born three weeks before Bert's death, and I just wanted to get on with my life and so I didn't bother to take him to court and sue him over the songs I didn't get. So I just let it go."

These fragments only became officially available in 1994, and for all one's sympathies with Bert Berns' widow, there is a certain ghoulish fascination in hearing Morrison originals such as 'Shake It Mable', 'You Say France And I Whistle' and 'Ring Worm'.

Full track listing, disc one: 'Brown Eyed Girl', 'He Ain't Give You None', 'T. B. Sheets', 'Spanish Rose', 'Goodbye Baby (Baby Goodbye)', 'Ro Ro Rosey', 'Who Drove The Red Sports Car', 'Midnight Special', 'Beside You', 'It's All Right', 'Madame George', 'Send Your Mind', 'The Smile You Smile', 'The Back Room', 'Joe Harper Saturday Morning', 'Chick-A-Boom', 'I Love You (The Smile You Smile)', 'Brown Eyed Girl' (alt.); disc two: 'Twist And Shake', 'Shake And Roll', 'Stomp And Scream', 'Scream And Holler', 'Jump And Thump', 'Drivin' Wheel', 'Just Ball', 'Make It Mable', 'Hold On George', 'The Big Royalty Check', 'Ring Worm', 'Savoy Hollywood', 'Freaky If You Got This Far', 'Up Your Mind', 'Thirty Two', 'All The Bits', 'You Say France And I Whistle', 'Blow In Your Nose', 'Nose In Your Blow', 'La Mambo', 'Go For Yourself', 'Want A Danish', 'Here Comes Dumb George', 'Chickee Coo', 'Do It, Hang On Groovy', 'Goodbye George', 'Dum Dum George', 'Walk And Talk', 'The Wobble', 'Wobbe And Ball'.

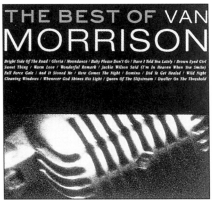

THE BEST OF VAN
MORRISON

Bright Side Of The Road / Gloria / Moondance / Baby Please Don't Go / Have I Told You Lately / Brown Eyed Girl
Sweet Thing / Warm Love / Wonderful Remark / Jackie Wilson Said (I'm In Heaven When You Smile)
Full Force Gale / And It Stoned Me / Here Comes The Night / Domino / Did Ye Get Healed / Wild Night
Cleaning Windows / Whenever God Shines His Light / Queen Of The Slipstream / Dweller On The Threshold

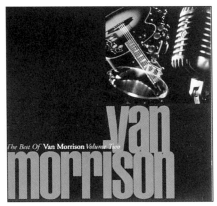

The Best Of **Van Morrison** *Volume Two*

van
morrison

THE BEST OF VAN MORRISON

(POLYDOR 841 970–2, MARCH 1990)

Everyone quibbles about what's left off their favourite act's Greatest Hits, but the compilers of 'The Best Of Van Morrison' got it pretty much on the mark. There were the recent hits ('Have I Told You Lately', 'Whenever God Shines His Light'), Them favourites ('Gloria' and 'Here Comes The Night') and long–time solo Van favourites ('Moondance', 'Brown Eyed Girl', 'Jackie Wilson Said', 'Domino', 'Warm Love'...). It was a radio-friendly, audience-expanding collection, and it worked, to the extent that soon after its release it provided Van with his first ever British Top 10 album.

Real fans bought it for the inclusion of the hard-to-get, 'Wonderful Remark'. Robbie Robertson had put together the soundtrack to Martin Scorsese's 1982 film *King Of Comedy,* in which 'Wonderful Remark' played over the end credits. Robert De Niro played the unfeasibly unappealing Rupert Pupkin, a man so desperate for fame that he kidnaps creepy chat show host Jerry Lewis. Reports had Morrison seething at the way the De Niro character was portrayed as a hero, because "he hadn't paid his dues". One of the most powerful Morrison songs of the period, 'Wonderful Remark' had only previously appeared on the US soundtrack album of the film.

"Some Other Rainbow" is a line from 'Wonderful Remark', which John McCarthy & Jill Morrell took as the title for their autobiography. McCarthy tells of how much Morrison's music sustained him during his captivity in Beirut, and that it was discussing Van's music with fellow hostage Brian Keenan that kept him sane. Keenan had been a neighbour of the Morrisons in Belfast, and his house used to be on Van's window–cleaning route.

It was McCarthy & Morrell who awarded Van with his Lifetime Achievement Award at The Brits ceremony in 1994. Among the acts paying tribute to Van at the occasion were Bob Dylan, Sting, Bono and Elvis Costello. A short set concluded the evening, made notable when Shane MacGowan accompanied Van on 'Gloria'.

Full track listing: 'Bright Side Of the Road', 'Gloria', 'Moondance', 'Baby Please Don't Go', 'Have I Told You Lately', 'Brown Eyed Girl', 'Sweet Thing', 'Warm Love', 'Wonderful Remark', 'Jackie Wilson Said (I'm In Heaven When You Smile)', 'Full Force Gale', 'Stoned Me', 'Here Comes The Night', 'Domino', 'Did Ye Get Healed', 'Wild Night', 'Cleaning Windows', 'Whenever God Shines His Light', 'Queen Of The Slipstream', 'Dweller On The Threshold'.

THE BEST OF VAN MORRISON VOLUME TWO

(POLYDOR 517 760-2, JANUARY 1993)

No surprises on this pointless sequel. Nothing new or hard to get, which was reflected in the album's nominal sales.

Full track listing: 'Real Real Gone', 'When Will I Ever Learn To Live In God', 'Sometime I Feel Like A Motherless Child', 'In The Garden', 'A Sense Of Wonder', 'I'll Tell Me Ma', 'Coney Island', 'Enlightenment', 'Rave On John Donne'/'Rave On Part 2 (Live)', 'Don't Look Back', 'It's All Over Now Baby Blue', 'One Irish Rover', 'The Mystery', 'Hymns To The Silence', 'Evening Meditation'.

ODDS & ENDS

A 1974 single 'Caledonia' with 'What's Up Crazy Pup' on its B-side has never been made available on album. You can understand Van's fondness for the A-side, if only for its title, while musically his cover of this 40s swing–style romp, pre–empts his later jazz fascination. 'Crazy Pup' is a Van original, very much in the style of Louis Jordan.

Even by the standards of a man whose career has always seen bizarre go hand-in-hand with genius, 'Mechanical Bliss' makes odd seem straightforward. The B-side of 1977's 'Joyous Sound', it's a shuffling piano, bass and drums ensemble, fronted by Van "rapping" in a voice like that of an irate *Daily Telegraph* reader. It sounds like the sort of thing a young George Ivan might have created on his first tape recorder, after years spent listening to BBC Light Entertainment programmes like *The Goons* and *Take It From Here*, all Ponsonby-Smythe and silly voices, ending with Van pronouncing: "OK chaps, stiff upper lip".

Robin Williamson's 'Mr Thomas' came on the B-side of 1983's 'Celtic Swing', a driving riff with a feisty Van vocal, and an inscrutable lyric concerning exile and a fondness for the eponymous Welsh poet, ending with "why don't we feel the way we're supposed to feel?"

Into the Nineties, Van Morrison's multiple CD single releases came with live versions of album favourites, including 'And The Healing Has Begun', 'See Me Through', 'It Fills You Up', 'Cleaning Windows'...

Following his switch to Warner Bros and the release of 'Astral Weeks', Morrison's solo career had taken off. He had no need to busk around for work, and rarely appeared on other people's albums, although during the Seventies, he made guest appearances on albums by John Lee Hooker, Sammy Hagar, Bill Wyman and, most importantly, The Band.

THE LAST WALTZ
(WARNER BROS 3146-2, 1978)

The Band's final show at San Francisco's Winterland Ballroom in late 1976. It was a rare Morrison appearance between 'Veedon Fleece' and 'A Period Of Transition', but this was too good an opportunity for Van to miss. As well as paying homage to his friends The Band, and acknowledging their influence on his own work, it also gave Van a chance to share the spotlight with some of the most luminous names in rock'n'roll - Bob Dylan, Eric Clapton, Neil Young, Ringo Starr, Joni Mitchell, Muddy Waters. Prior to Live Aid, The Last Waltz was long felt to be the most glittering array of rock stars ever assembled.

Morrison's contributions on the three album, 2CD souvenir, were a duet with The Band's throaty Richard Manuel on the old chestnut 'Tura Lura Lura (That's An Irish Lullaby)', and his own 'Caravan'. For many though, the highlight of the subsequent film directed by Martin Scorsese (which many still

regard as the definitive rock concert film), is Van high-stepping his way through 'Caravan'. It is a steaming Morrison tour-de-force, and, bless him, the ungainly Tiller Girl routine only makes you want to love him all the more.

THE WALL –
LIVE IN BERLIN
(MERCURY 8466112, 1990)

Van was an incongruous guest at Roger Waters' ambitious re-staging of Pink Floyd's 'The Wall' at the Berlin Wall in 1989, a massive event which welcomed glasnost and celebrated the end of Communism. Along with Waters, who wrote the bulk of the double album for Pink Floyd a decade before, Van contributed some storming lead vocals on 'Comfortably Numb'. Alongside Van, the other star guests included Sinead O'Connor, Bryan Adams, Joni Mitchell and Cyndi Lauper.

NO PRIMA DONNA: THE SONGS OF VAN MORRISON

(EXILE 523368-2, AUGUST 1994)

When no one got together to record the long-overdue tribute album to Van Morrison, Van decided to kickstart the whole thing himself.

The tribute album thing was big business during the Nineties – by the time Van's homage was released, we had already witnessed tributes to Richard Thompson, Leonard Cohen, George Gershwin, The Carpenters, Curtis Mayfield... It was a nice idea: the disciples paying heartfelt homage to their soul and inspiration.

Except that something went horribly wrong with 'No Prima Donna'. As an influence, Van had been cited as formative by everyone from Dexy's Midnight Runners and The Waterboys, through to The Pogues, The Proclaimers and U2 – but where were they when they were needed? 'No Prima Donna' had its share of familiar faces like Brian Kennedy, Sinead O'Connor and Phil Coulter, But the absences were notable, the choice of material too left-field, and the project never seemed to really catch fire.

There were undeniable highlights – Liam Neeson's reading of 'Coney Island' was every bit as strong as you'd expect from an Oscar-nominated actor and long-time Van fan; Elvis Costello's acapella 'Full Force Gale' with The Voice Squad hit the mark; and Cassandra Wilson's version of 'Crazy Love' was warm and sensuous...

For me though, the highlight of 'No Prima Donna' was Marianne Faithfull's handling of 'Madame George'. It wasn't just because – as you may have guessed – it's Van's best song, it was the fact that La Faithfull put herself into the song, and made it her own in the world-weary, smoky voice of Marlene Dietrich as Shanghai Lil. Marianne sings it as 'Madame Joy', which is how Van always intended it. She told me in 1994 that 'Astral Weeks' was one of her

"favourite stoned albums in the Sixties...
I always thought that Van says 'Madame
Joy', and he really does sing 'Madame
Joy'... You see the title and it says
'Madame George' – but he sings
'Madame Joy'. So I bounced in to him
and said 'You sing 'Madame Joy' don't
you? Can I sing that?' 'Yeah, awright'".

Van fans got very excited when July
1996 was earmarked for the release of
the double CD, 'The Philosopher's
Stone'. A catalogue number and release
date were confirmed, the press release
promised "the first ever collection of
unreleased tracks from Van Morrison".
The 30 tracks promised, recorded
between 1971 and 1988, were a real
treasure trove for Morrison collectors:
early versions of 'Wonderful Remark',
'Real Real Gone', 'Bright Side Of The
Road'; covers of 'Foggy Mountain Top'
and 'John Brown's Body' as well as a
cornucopia of wonderful others.

The set has now been postponed
until 1997, so that Van can concentrate
on his Mose Allison tribute album, 'Tell
Me Something', which is pencilled in for

a late 1996 release. Van has also been
working with rock'n'roll legend Carl
Perkins on a new album during 1996.

Journalist Mick Brown remembers
working with Van for a BBC TV show.
Things were going fine, Van was co-
operative during rehearsal, but as soon
as the cameras were on and Brown
repeated his first question, Morrison
replied: "You must be mad if you think
I'm going to answer that!" Much later,
Morrison stonewalled another question
with: "Nobody asks a bricklayer about
laying bricks. Why ask about writing
songs? There's no difference. I just do
what I do."

Bless him. Long may he keep
laying bricks.